DUCKTAILS

by Janette Oke

Illustrated by
Brenda Mann

Dedicated with love
to the children
of our Sunday School class at
St. Mark Missionary Church.
May God bless you.

Table of Contents

Chapter One

New Beginnings

It was warm and cozy in the shell. Most of the time I lay, tightly curled up, in complete silence and stillness, but every now and then there would be stirring from some strange unseen and unknown something or someone from the outside and I would be moved this way or that. Faint sounds would reach me. Often it was only the sound of the stirring up of the nest, but at times it was as though someone above me was trying to communicate.

There was nothing exciting about my existence. I slept, I was nourished, and I knew that I grew, for daily my warm, protective, tightly worn, little home was getting smaller. I began to push out against it but it would not give.

One day I awoke to more movement. I was turned over again, and I didn't like the new position. It made me even more conscious of how tight my confining home had become. I pushed harder against it but nothing happened. I could not even move to get leverage. For one moment I felt a bit of panic and I struck out again. I found that I could move my head, ever so slightly, and because it was the only thing that I could move, and because there was a beak on it that could strike against things, I began to peck and poke away at the walls that were holding me tightly, hoping to make more room for myself.

For awhile it seemed that I got nowhere. If only I wasn't bundled up so tightly so that I could get a better swing with my bill. Still, I did not give up. I kept poking and pecking, trying to make the enclosure back up a bit. I soon had to stop and rest. It wore me out and my effort seemed to be accomplishing nothing.

I slept for a while and when I awoke, I started all over again—peck, peck. I rested and then worked, again and again. It was a long, difficult, awkward job and just as I was beginning to despair, there was a soft cracking sound and a small break appeared where my beak had been pounding. I took heart and kept at my work. I still had to rest often. I was so confined that even my small effort easily tired me, but I was making headway. The break was getting bigger and bigger.

When I would stop to rest I could often hear stirrings and peckings around me. It seemed that there were others who were also trying to break free from a similar bondage. The thought filled me with excitement and I went back to work again with a more determined effort.

Gradually the opening was getting a little wider and a little wider. I could move my head more freely now and I worked until I was in an exhausted frenzy. I was so anxious to be free. I didn't know what would greet me outside of my warm protective home, but I was eager to find out.

At last it happened. The whole roof toppled from me and rolled aside. I untucked my head from where it had been secured beneath my wing and fought to open my eyes against the strangeness of the soft light that seeped into the nest from various uncovered corners.

The stirrings were near at hand now and very easy to detect. I could not only hear them but I could feel them too. All around me was activity. Nearby were smooth, oval eggs that matched the likeness of my one-time home. Here and there within the nest were struggling small creatures who, like me, were trying desperately to free themselves of the shell. I spotted one fellow who had accomplished the task completely. He laid on his stomach, stretching and pushing and trying to get his feet under him.

"I made it," I heard him say and he seemed quite pleased with himself.

Just as he said it, another little creature gave one last desperate push and toppled over against him, landing on his back. They righted themselves and began to gleefully giggle at the fact that they were free. Others, like me, still struggled. The one next to me had only succeeded in getting a small hole poked in the side of the shell. I wanted to call encouragement to him but I didn't know what to say and I was still out of breath from my big push.

I still had a ways to go until I would be free like the other two. After a short rest, I began pushing against the bottom of the shell again with my feet and flapping about with the rest of my body, wriggling and squirming and trying to break loose. I worked with all of my might. The efforts paid off, and suddenly I felt myself fall free from the shell and tumble onto a brother who was still struggling.

I lay there panting. What a strange feeling to be able to move! It was exhilarating. As soon as I caught my breath I tried it again. I flapped the stub of a wing. Though there was room for it to move now, it was a clumsy effort on my part. I just didn't seem to be able to get the appendage under proper control. It flapped crazily, thumping another small creature on the side and making him complain. I tried my feet. Yes, they moved too, though they didn't seem to move in the direction that I wanted them to. I pushed myself forward. I scooted on my tummy and ran headlong into a struggling egg. Just then another creature came bumping into me, giggling as she tipped me over. I struggled to right myself again and pushed myself back onto my stomach and tried to get my feet under me. She was still beside me.

"Hi", she said.

I turned my head so that I could look at her. "Hi," I answered. "What are you?"

She giggled again. "I don't know—yet," she stated, "but I like it. I think that it's going to be fun."

I thought so, too.

I tried to move again and only managed to flop forward. I looked down at my gangly feet.

"I think that they're supposed to work better than this," I said to the nearby creature.

"Why do you say that?" she asked me. "Mine work just fine. I couldn't even move a few moments ago and now look."

She gave a big push forward and toppled into another creature and laughed again.

"See," she called to me, "I can move."

I gave another push and though I too was pleased that I could move, I still had no direction and no control. I clung stubbornly to my first thought. *It should work better than this.*

All around us there was movement. Little creatures flopped awkwardly here and there, pushing this way and that. They seemed to enjoy it, though it was certainly uncontrolled and misguided.

"Push harder!" I heard an excited cry as someone called encouragement to one who was still struggling. Then there was a little cracking sound and the new one, too, broke free.

It was all very exhausting—the effort, the excitement, the newness of it all. I was soon so tired that I knew that I just had to get some sleep. I tucked my head back under my wing, where it had been for so many days, and which seemed the most natural place for it to be, snuggled down against a warm fluffy body next to me and slept.

Chapter Two

Family

When I awoke there was much activity around me. The warm sun streamed in from above making it hard for me to open my eyes. The downy soft covering was gone from above us. We were exposed to a vast, new and very big world.

I struggled to my feet and looked about me. They worked a little better now. I could even lift my body up a bit so that when I wanted to I could move forward in a different fashion than pushing along on my tummy.

"Isn't it wonderful!" said a voice beside me. It was her again.

I looked up. It was so far up. It seemed that there was just no top to this world, it was so very far away.

I looked around me. We were in the nest. There were a number of us. The others all looked alike. I looked down at myself to see if I looked like them, too. I wasn't sure.

"Hey," I said, turning to the voice beside me, "Do I look like you?"

She giggled. "I don't know. I don't know what I look like."

That didn't seem to help much.

I looked around again and then I got another idea. "Well, do I look like them?"

She looked around us.

"Yes. Just like them."

It was nice to hear. At least I was among my own kind— whatever we were.

"Then we are the same." I spoke softly with great relief in my voice but she heard me.

"Good," she said. "Then we are family."

"Family?" I puzzled. "What's family?"

"I don't know," she admitted, "but I heard someone talking and they said that we are family. I think that it's good."

I was relieved to hear that it was good, but it still didn't explain what it was.

I looked about me again. There was only one more egg to go. The creature who was struggling to free itself from it was working feverishly and those nearby were busy cheering him on.

Soon we would all be out of the confining shells and into the 'family' nest. *What happens next?* I wondered. As soon as we are all free, what happens next?

I wasn't to wonder for long for, at that moment, someone very big and very different from us suddenly appeared. She had been standing close by. She reached down a long neck and spoke to us.

"Hello children," she said and there was love in her voice. "You are all here. That's nice. It's so good to see you. We've been waiting a long time."

Now I was really confused. She had called us 'children.'

"I thought that we were family" I said, not wanting to be cheeky, but anxious to get things understood.

"Oh, you are," she quickly assured me. "I am your mother and you are my children, and that makes us family."

"Wow!" I exclaimed. "That's so much to sort out."

She smiled right at me, just as though I was the only one in the nest. "You'll soon have it all figured out," she assured me.

She talked to some of the others then, saying words of

greeting and love and nuzzling them with her long, orange bill.

The last little one broke free of the shell just then and a cry of celebration went up from the cheering section on that side of the nest. We all were free.

Our big-creature mother looked pleased too. "You're all here," she said again happily. "All nine of you. I can hardly wait for your father to see you."

"Father?" I asked curiously.

"Yes, your father. He's part of the family too."

"Is he like us?" the little voice beside me asked before I could even ask it.

"Oh my, no," said our mother. "He is much bigger than you. He is even bigger than me."

There were gasps from the nest. We couldn't imagine someone even bigger than our mother.

"You should sleep now," said Mother. "You've all had a very busy day."

She arranged us in the nest and moved over us. Her warm, fluffy body was lowered ever so gently to cover us with her soft feathers. The bright sun was blotted out and we soon began to feel the warmth of her and of one another. I felt very sleepy. I curled my head under my wing again and slept.

"Wake up, wake up," Mother was saying. "Your father's here. He's anxious to meet you."

I opened my eyes. A big creature, who looked much like Mother, was bending over us, looking very pleased. Carefully he surveyed us, counting each one. Perhaps he counted all of our wings and feet, too, I didn't know. I just knew that he studied us and seemed content with what he found.

"This is your father," Mother said again.

"Hello there," said the big creature. "I'm glad that you have all arrived safely."

Mother began her introductions. "This is Boyd, and Hiram, Prudence, Hazel, Gertrude, and Oscar. And this is Fluff," she said indicating the tiny, giggling one, "and this is Zackery," she nodded her head at the one who stood so very close to me with a twinkle in his eye. And then she turned to me. "And this is Quackery."

'Quackery!' So that was me!

"Quackery," giggled the little one. "Quackery. That's a funny name."

I remembered that her name had been Fluff. Yes, to a Fluff, Quackery might sound pretty funny.

I turned to the one named Zackery and nodded an acknowledgement. It seemed to me that he had far more sense than the giggling creature.

"Hey," he said, his eyes still twinkling, "our names rhyme— Zackery and Quackery."

I liked him, this new brother. I had a feeling that we'd get along just fine, but before I had a chance to get fully acquainted Mother was stirring us up again.

"Come on now. It's time to be up and on our way. We have much to learn."

The whole nest was stirring—all nine of us.

"First you need to learn how to eat," Mother continued.

"Eat?" I had never heard of eating.

"Follow me," urged Mother and she left the nest and we scrambled to follow her.

It was only one small step for Mother to leave the nest but it was like crossing a mountain to the rest of us. We struggled up the steep slope, pushing with our feet as well as with our short, stubby wings. It was hard going up and messy work coming down. One by one we reached the edge of the long climb up and then went sprawling down on the other side as we tried to make the descent.

We gathered ourselves from the dust and scrambled to our feet and hurried after Mother.

Our feet were working better now, though occasionally they still let us down and we would go tumbling forward onto our tummy or right onto our neck and we would have to give a quick push, our face in the dirt, to fight our way back on our feet again.

We reached an area where all kinds of creatures milled about. Some strutted, some waddled or tumbled like us, and others just seemed to float along. I looked about curiously. It was rather frightening. Was it safe to go in there?

But Father did not hesitate. He walked right into the midst of the bunch with Mother following closely behind him. We had been told to follow, so, reluctantly, we moved forward also.

We came to a container with something in it.

"This is water," Mother said. "We all need water in order to live."

She put her bill in the water and then lifted her long neck upward and stretched her bill in the air. Something along her neck sort of bounced. Father did the same thing.

"Now you try it," he said. "You fill your bill with the water and then lift your head high and swallow."

We tried. Most of us tumbled forward into the water and flopped about on our tummies in our effort to get out again. It wasn't as easy as it looked. It was wet. We got up shaking the drops of water from our downy feathers, not sure if we liked the feel of it. We tried again. It seemed that our bills just wouldn't go down without the rest of us following.

It took several tries before I was able to get a little of the water where it belonged—down my throat. Once I had caught on, I rather liked the feel and the taste of it. I drank more. I was not good at it, but I was learning.

We moved on from the water to an area where the ground was covered with little round things.

"Now you must eat," said Mother.

At first I had no idea as to what we were to do. Mother and Father tried to show us.

"Like this," said Mother, and pecked at the ground.

"Like this," I repeated and pecked at the ground, too.

My sister giggled and followed our example.

It was hard for me to understand. What was so special about 'eating'? Then I noticed that Father and Mother weren't just pecking at the ground. When they lifted their beaks they actually had something in them. Bits of something lay scattered all over the ground and they were busy picking them up. I decided to follow their example. I picked one up. It fell before I could even lift it. I tried again. Again I lost it. I chose a smaller one and tried again. On my fifth try with the smaller one I was able to lift it from the ground. *What do I do with it now?* I watched Father to see but when I lifted my head to observe him I lost it again and had to start all over.

It was some time before I got the hang of it, but soon I discovered that I could actually lift one with regularity. I ran about in my excitement picking them up and laying them down. I still couldn't understand why this was such an important thing to achieve. Besides, my tummy was beginning to hurt.

"No. No. Not like that," Mother said softly. "You eat it. Like this."

She reached down, took a bite off the ground, held it securely in her bill and then, with a quick outward motion of her long neck, the piece disappeared. She had swallowed it! It was amazing.

I picked up a small piece, held it securely aloft, gave my neck a quick little twitch—and lost it. I had to try again and again. Finally I got it to work. I went on then, picking up more pieces and swallowing them. A strange thing happened. Gradually my tummy stopped hurting. I was feeling quite comfortable and even getting sleepy. I noticed that the others began to look like I was feeling. I heard my father and mother talking.

"Perhaps that is long enough for their first outing," my father was saying.

Mother looked about. "I think you're right," she said. "They look tired. Let's take them home."

They called to us then and we tumbled along behind them and scurried back to our nest. It was a long, difficult climb to get back to the nest again. Mother and Father often had to assist one or the other of us by giving us a helpful boost with their long bills. One by one we tumbled into the nest and lay exhausted on the softness of the bottom. It was so good to be home. It was good to be able to rest our tired little bodies. It was even good to feel the comforting warmth of Mother's softness, though the day had not been cold.

We snuggled down, put our heads under our wings and cuddled up together. So much had happened in the last few hours that I couldn't believe how my world had changed. I could hardly wait for more discoveries, but for now I was too tired to even think about it. I shut my eyes and let sleep come.

Chapter Three

Lessons

It had been a busy day and now my tummy was full and I was satisfied. I slept well, but it seemed that I hadn't been sleeping for long when we were awakened and stirred up again.

"Come," Mother was saying.

"But I'm not hungry yet," I protested sleepily.

She laughed at me. "Well, we do have things to do besides eat," she said. "It's time to go to the pond."

"The pond?"

"You'll see. Come on sleepyhead."

She stepped off the nest and called to us to follow and we struggled out again. It was still a big climb even though my legs felt much stronger and steadier. We tumbled out one by one, following the lead of our father and mother.

I didn't look back once I had left the nest and started my fast, tumbling descent down the other side. I could hear Mother scolding gently the last two or three to leave the nest. "Come on, Hazel. And you, Hiram. You mustn't keep the rest of the family waiting. Hurry now."

I hastened to keep up with my father. Zackery was panting along at my side and Fluff was not far behind us.

"Wait for me," she cried as she tried to catch up.

We looked at one another in impatience, but we did stop and wait for her and she came scurrying along to join us, her little wings flapping in her effort to speed herself along.

Father slowed down so that it would be easier for us to keep pace and I could hear Mother still urging on the stragglers at the end of the little brigade.

We tumbled along, trying hard to keep up to our father as told. I knew that he was considering us and could have traveled much faster than he did. At times he even hesitated and waited for us, giving us a chance to catch up a bit. Just as I began to hope for a little rest, he would begin walking again.

At last we reached a very strange looking thing. It lay out before us, shimmering in the morning sun. I could see the grasses and trees that grew along its sides, right there in the thing itself. I wondered if they grew down, as well as up.

Father waited until we had gathered around him and then he did a very strange thing. He left the solid ground and walked right out into the thing called the 'pond.' It came up on his legs instead of letting him walk on top of it, first covering his feet, and then with the next step, coming up almost to his body.

I thought that he would soon disappear from sight but just as he stepped forward again, he sat, right on the water and he began to move slowly forward. Then he circled and came back toward us.

I stood with my mouth open, watching him. How did he do that?

"Go on," urged Mother. "Follow your father."

I was anxious to try it and would have gladly plunged in but Prudence was standing in my way.

"It'll go right over my head," she wailed. "Father's big, but I'll-I'll just disappear."

"Nonsense," laughed Mother. "You will swim just like your father. Now go on. Try it."

Still Prudence balked. I scrambled around her and put my

foot into the wetness, testing it. *Dare I try it? Will I really float on the top?*

I took another step and held my breath. It worked! I was still on top of the water even though my feet could no longer touch ground. It was amazing.

My father circled around beside me. He was smiling at me.

"Good," he said. "Now give a push—like this, your foot against the water."

He demonstrated.

I followed his example and gave a push and to my great surprise, I moved forward. I gave another hard push, and another, and ran smack into a cluster of reeds.

I could hear Father chuckling softly. He reached out his long bill and pulled me back gently.

"You need to learn to use both feet," he told me. "That way you can learn to steer. If you want to turn this way, you push hard with this foot. If you want to turn this way, you push with this foot."

I tried it. It really did work. It took me a while to get it working just right but when I did, it was fun, I loved it.

Zackery was beside me now.

"Look," I called to him. "I'm doing it. Look."

The others all joined us and were swimming around the entrance to the pond in various stages of proficiency. There were calls and cries of excitement. It seemed that all of us felt good about the water.

Mother finally managed to coax Prudence in and she too found that she didn't sink right to the bottom. Even she seemed to enjoy herself, though she was much more cautious than the rest of us.

Fluff was giggling again. "I can do it. Just look at me. I can do it."

"Now," said Mother when the excitement died down some, "follow us," and she led the way and the rest of us sped up our swiftly kicking little feet so that we could follow.

At first we swam slowly around the pond—slowly for Mother and Father, that is. The rest of us had to work quite hard at it. Father and Mother checked on us frequently and sometimes offered advice or correction on our stroke or our steering.

Prudence still swam stiffly as though she feared that the water might suddenly change its mind and decide to put her under.

"Loosen up dear," I heard Mother say to her. "Just relax and let the water hold you. Like this. Come on, relax. Trust it."

Prudence loosened up some but she did not relax.

We moved on farther, slowly moving in and out of the reeds and water plants.

"Now," said Father, "we taught you how to find food in the farmyard. Today we are going to teach you how to find food in the water."

I looked around me for scattered grain but saw none.

"The water is full of tasty things," Father went on. "You just need to know how to look for them. Watch closely."

And with those words, both Father and Mother began to point out things that were good to eat. The food floated on the surface of the water or concealed itself under the leaves of the growing things. We soon learned to spot it. It was great fun to see who could find it first and we all rushed to catch it when we spotted something that was good to eat.

Mother and Father seemed pleased with our quickness in learning. Only Hazel complained.

"I never get any," she whined. "By the time I get there it's already gone."

"Then you must learn to be faster," said Mother. But Hazel responded with, "I can't. They won't wait for me. You find it for me Mother."

Mother did find her one or two delicious bugs and then she insisted that Hazel, like the rest of us, do her own looking.

Every now and then Father or Mother would look about and take count to make sure that all of us were gathered around them. If some of us strayed a bit far or lagged too far behind, we were called to get back together with the rest of the family. Hiram was the one that needed admonition the most frequently. He always seemed to be lagging.

After we had fully mastered the art of finding food from the surface of the pond, Father decided that it was time for another lesson.

"Now, you have learned of all the good things on the pond surface. Now we will show you what else we are able to do." And with those words he gave a quick flip and disappeared completely from our sight. We all gasped. Amazing!

As the minutes ticked by slowly, we all began to be concerned. Prudence even began to cry. She was sure that Father was lost. I looked inquiringly at Mother. She did not appear to be worried. I felt a measure of reassurance, but even I wished that he would soon appear again. How could he stay under the water for such a long, long time?

At last he reappeared and smiled at all of us. He had something in his bill and from the look on his face I judged that it must be something especially tasty.

"Your turn Mother," he said, and while he watched our

concerned and anxious faces, Mother disappeared from sight and remained under the gentle swells of water.

She didn't stay as long as Father had. Perhaps she knew that we were still uncertain about it all. When she surfaced, she too had a morsel of something to eat in her bill. She seemed to enjoy it as she ate it slowly.

"Now it's your turn," said Father. I couldn't believe that he meant that we would actually be able to *do* that.

"Watch carefully," he went on. "This is how it is done."

He proceeded to demonstrate to us the ease and skill of diving.

I was anxious to get started. The first time that I tried, I just

bobbed quickly to the surface again. I tried again. It seemed that I just couldn't get my little body under the surface of the water. At last I managed to correct my position and under I went.

It was truly amazing. There were all kinds of things to see under the water. Zackery was there beside me. He gave a whoop and choked on the water that he inhaled. He had to resurface to catch his breath and then he was under again. All around us were kicking, struggling legs and diving bodies. We could still hear Prudence complaining to Mother that she didn't want to try to touch the bottom and Zackery made as though to pull her underneath the surface of the water but I shook my head at him. As nervous as Prudence was about swimming, I was afraid that she might never try diving if given a fright by Zackery.

Each time that I went under, I had to return quickly to the surface for air. I couldn't even reach the floor of the pond where all of the good things seemed to be. Father swished down past me, found and chose something, picked it up and resurfaced again. I went back up for a good gulp of air and determined to follow his leading. I still didn't make it to the bottom. It seemed to be such a very long way. I tried again and again but I never did make it. I did enjoy the diving though, and Zackery and I were soon feeling that we were quite good at it.

Fluff tried hard to imitate every move that we made, but being smaller and not as strong, she often came short of what we dared.

We spent much of our morning on the pond. Other creatures joined us. We were curious about them, but they spent their time on one side and we spent our time on the other side. Father and Mother did bid them a 'good morning' but that was the only exchange. They were much too busy with their families for any visiting to be done.

Long before we were ready to go, Father called and said that we should return to the farmyard. We were reluctant to go but we knew that we must follow.

As we walked to the farmyard, Hiram tagging along at the end of the line, I was far more curious about the creatures that we saw than I had been before. On the previous outing it had been all that I could do to make my short legs move in proper fashion. Now, though I still stumbled occasionally, they really worked quite well, though I had to admit that it was much easier to maneuver in the water than out on the ground.

We found the water dish and Mother and Father took a brief drink just to remind us how it was done. I remembered, but I wasn't thirsty. I had drank from the pond all morning just for the fun of it.

We moved on to the scattered grain. I pecked and poked some. In fact I was a bit hungry. Zackery and I had been far too busy playing in the water of the pond to do much feeding. I soon settled down to the business of filling my rather empty tummy.

"Can we swim again?" I heard Zackery coaxing.

Father laughed.

"Didn't you get your fill?" he asked.

"No, oh no," said Zackery. "I loved it. Can we go again?"

"We'll all go again. Often," said Father, "but not right now. Right now it is time for a rest."

"But I'm not tired," persisted Zackery.

"But some of your brothers and sisters are," reminded Father. "They need a rest before another swim."

I looked about at the rest of the family. Some of them did look tired. In fact Hazel was lying down with a wing over her head, shutting out the sun and the noise as she tried to catch some sleep. She wasn't even bothering to eat.

"Come," called Mother. "It's time for a rest."

One by one we gathered behind her and started off to the nest, Father bringing up the rear and urging the slower ones on.

The climb back into the nest wasn't nearly as difficult. We tumbled in, a bit out of breath and snuggled down together. I hadn't realized how tired I was until I felt the warm feathers of Mother's body against me. I closed my eyes then and cuddled up against Zackery and Fluff for a much needed sleep.

Chapter Four

Growing Up

We swam again in the afternoon. Zackery and I were beginning to feel very confident in our ability. We loved it and soon began to play games of daring and skill. With Fluff acting as our timekeeper or our judge, we would dive and see which one of us could stay under the longest or dive the deepest or swim the farthest under water. Sometimes we got so busy playing games that we forgot to eat and then we felt hungry when we should have been well fed.

In the days that followed we spent our time in much the same way as we had our first day at the pond. Our swimming skills increased and I soon was able to dive all the way to the bottom. We still continued our times of fun and daring. Zackery and I loved to try to outdo one another.

Sometimes our brothers and sisters joined in the games—at least some of them did. Oscar was the biggest and strongest member of the family and he always seemed to be able to beat us. We didn't ask Oscar to join us very often for we did not like to be beaten. Our only escape from Oscar taking over our games was the fact that he had a tremendous appetite and was always so busy eating that he didn't have much time to join in the play.

Hazel never cared to join the games. It took far too much energy, and energy seemed to be one thing that Hazel was short of. She floated about lazily picking bugs off the surface of the pond, not even caring to dive any more than she had to. Prudence usually joined her, for though Prudence was not lazy, she was timid and she didn't like to do anything that took some daring. She didn't care much for diving either. She always seemed to be afraid that she might meet something under the water that she didn't care for. Mother tried to coax her, telling her that under the water was her place of safety and that she, like the rest of the family, must be prepared to dive and to dive without a moment's hesitation should danger ever present itself.

Prudence looked nervous about the whole thing, but she did not practice her diving.

Meanwhile Zackery and I, with Fluff close behind, began to do a little experimenting and exploring on our own.

With the passing of the days, we were soon able to reach the bottom of the pond with no trouble at all. We not only fed on the bottom but we played games on the bottom as well.

Zackery was usually the one to think them up, but I was always willing to try them. Once, in following Zackery's lead in a game of follow-the-leader, I became entangled in a mesh of weeds at the bottom and probably would still be there had it not been for the quick thinking of Fluff who alerted my father. With a thrust of his strong bill he loosened the weeds that bound me and I scurried to the top of the pond and some much needed gulps of air.

Father scolded us and warned us not to take foolish chances underwater, or anywhere for that matter, and for a few days our games were more cautious. But we soon forgot the warning and went back to taking our risks.

We got to be very good swimmers and loved to spend our time in the water. I think that Zackery would have been willing to sleep there had not Father insisted that we return to the nest each night.

We were growing. Oscar was still our biggest family member and Fluff our smallest, but we were all growing. We were all getting more co-ordinated too. We never tumbled forward on our faces anymore as we scrambled along trying to keep pace with Father and Mother, and Father did not even have to shorten his stride much anymore.

We spent our days on the pond, with trips to the farmyard for grain, and our nights back in the nest. Our bodies were stronger and our minds more alert. Mother and Father still kept a watchful eye over us but we were allowed to swim out further and further from the rest of the family now, and our curiosity often led us to do just that.

Zackery and I began to wonder about the other occupants of the pond. Some of them looked like us, but there were some larger, white creatures that did not. They did not talk like us either and it took concentration for us to be able to understand them. We wished to get close enough to ask a few questions but just as we hoped that we could approach them, Father or Mother would call us back and set off in another direction. Zackery and I began to swing out a little closer and a little closer to where their family swam. We had one eye on Father and Mother as we did so and hoped that we would not be noticed. Just as we were getting close enough to be able to chat, Gertrude, who was always the one to observe an infraction and speak to Mother and Father about it, spoke up, "Zackery and Quackery are getting far away again," and Father's head came up and he called us back. "Keep with the family, boys," he ordered and we had to come back.

Zackery grumbled. "How are we ever going to learn anything if we can't even leave the family?" he complained.

I agreed with him, though I wasn't sure that I should voice it.

"Well, I'm not giving up," Zackery went on. "One of these times noisy Gertrude won't be looking."

He did not explain what he hoped to do then. I really didn't need to ask him. I would be ready to follow.

Our chance came the next afternoon. It seemed that some of the family members of our neighbor family were feeling the same way that we were for they too were swimming out in widening circles. I had one eye on Father and the other eye on Zackery as we swam about, getting a little farther and a little farther from our family and a little closer and a little closer to the other inhabitants of the pond, when suddenly there was a "swish" sound and a body surfaced right before our eyes.

It was another of our kind and very close to us. *Why hadn't we thought to do that,* I wondered. We too could have made good use of our ability to swim under water. We could swim a long ways now and could have gotten very near to the other family by using this trick.

"Hi," said the other fellow.

Zackery moved in closer. "Hi," he answered for us.

"Been watching you," said the other fellow.

"We've been watching you, too," I answered knowing that the other fellow was probably aware of that.

"What's your names?" he asked us then.

Zackery took over. "He's Quackery and I'm Zack," he said. I looked at this brother who had been so excited that our names rhymed. How come he was suddenly Zack? But Zackery paid no attention to my stare.

"My name's Clinton," he went on. "You can call me Clint. Do you live near the pond?"

I thought that it was rather a foolish question. I presumed that we *all* lived near the pond.

"Right over there," said Zackery, nodding his head in the direction from which we always came.

"Me too," said Clinton. "Maybe—"

But our conversation was interrupted by Clinton's folks who called first. We could hear them scolding him as he returned to the confining circle of the family.

Mother called then and we too were lightly reprimanded.

"Why is it wrong to talk to one of our kind?" I asked her, trying not to sound impudent, but wanting to know.

"It's not wrong to speak to one of our kind," she informed me. "We visit often with them, but not when we have a family to train and care for. When we are training our family, that comes first and takes all of our time and attention. And as long as you are in training, you stay with the family and learn the rules and the dangers. The others aren't ready to venture out yet—in fact, you and your brother need to learn more caution as well. This time you only spoke to those of our kind but it could have been someone who could have brought you harm. You must wait for our instructions before you make such moves."

I wondered if Zackery had been listening and if he would heed Mother's voice. It sounded logical to me. Mother had a legitimate point. We didn't know our friends from our enemies. We would do well to listen to Mother and Father and to take each step forward only as they saw us ready for it.

Chapter Five

Questions

We were changing. Among the soft fluff of our downy feathers, stiffer, darker feathers were coming in. We were growing up and Zackery and I took great pride in the fact.

"Soon we won't need to listen to Mother and Father anymore," said Zackery. "They are much too cautious anyway, I don't think that there *are* even enemies around here. I haven't seen any. Have you?"

"Well—no," I stammered. "But if they say—"

Gertrude overheard the conversation and quickly butted in. "You'd better behave or I'll tell Mother," she warned. "You're just asking for trouble. If Father and Mother say that there are enemies, then you can be sure—"

But Zackery cut in, his annoyance showing. "Why don't you just buzz off," he said angrily. "You're always being big-miss-bossy, telling everybody else how to live."

I was afraid that there was going to be a row but before it could really get started Father appeared and both of them wisely stopped. I knew that the fight would continue when Father was not around. I hoped that I wouldn't be around either. I did not find fights pleasant and tried to avoid them whenever possible.

"We are going to the farmyard for the evening feeding," Father said. "Everyone ready?"

I quickly fell into line, and Zackery, who was still angry, fell in beside me.

"She's so bossy," he grumbled.

"Ignore her then," I prompted.

"Ignore her? How can I ignore her? She's always there with her beak into everything."

I didn't want to get in an argument with Zackery so I held my tongue. "Maybe that new guy will be in the yard," I said to change the subject.

Zackery brightened some, but then he scowled. "What good will it do. They won't let us near enough to talk to him anyway."

"They might not mind in the yard. The water dishes and the grain are all quite close together. Everyone feeds in the same area."

Zackery seemed to think about that. It was true. We did all eat together—even with some of the creatures who were not our kind. No one seemed to think it strange to make any fuss about it whatever. I saw a smile replace Zackery's frown.

Just before we got to the yard, Zackery leaned forward and whispered in my ear, "Call me Zack, huh?"

I turned and looked at him. Now it was my turn to frown.

"Whatever for?" I asked, but before I could even finish, he said briskly, "I like it better, that's all."

I nodded.

It sounded pretty dumb to me but if that's what he wanted I'd call him Zack. But what about the rest of the family? I couldn't imagine Gertrude agreeing to call him Zack without a better reason than the one that Zackery had just given me. I did not mention Gertrude. It would just make Zackery—Zack—angry again.

When we got to the yard there were many others there

already feeding. I spotted Clinton almost immediately, and I guessed that Zackery did too, for I noticed that he was trying to work his way, inconspicuously, toward Clinton as we fed. Mother and Father did not seem to notice as they were busy searching out and devouring the scattered grain.

"Keep moving over toward that corner," Zack said to me. I was curious, too, about this new creature, and so I allowed myself to be guided slowly, steadily, toward the other side of the circle as we fed.

When we got within speaking distance, which didn't take too long as Clinton had been making his way toward us too, Zackery spoke softly, "Hi." Clinton answered back just as quietly, "Hi."

"How ya doing?" said Zackery—Zack.

"Great. How ya doing?"

"Good. Ya have a good swim today?" asked Zack.

"Yeah. We learned how to stay under for a long time."

"Quack and I already know that," boasted Zack.

I looked at him. It was one thing for him to insist upon being called Zack, it was quite another thing for him to decide to call me *Quack*. I didn't care much for the name but I didn't say anything.

"I was talking to one of the older guys," went on Clinton. "He says that we don't know anything about the fun of the pond. He says to just wait until a real good wind comes up. That's when swimming is fun. The waves lift you way up and then drop you way down. Just like a great big roller coaster— up and down just like that."

I wondered what a roller coaster was, but I didn't show my ignorance by asking.

"Boy, that sounds fun," Zack was saying. "I hope that the wind blows soon. I can hardly wait to try it."

"It's not too good on our pond," Clinton went on. "It's too sheltered. He says that the pond across the road gets much higher waves because it is bigger and more open to the wind."

We were forbidden to cross the road and, according to Father and Mother, so were the offspring of the other families.

"He's tried it?" asked Zack, his eyes big.

"Does it all the time," went on Clinton. "I'm gonna try it, too, the first chance that I get."

Just then there was a loud call. "Mother," yelled Gertrude in her loudest, most offensive voice, "Zackery and Quackery are off talking to strangers again."

I could feel the anger in Zackery. Not only had Gertrude brought us to the attention of our parents, but to every creature in the yard. It made us sound like little kids, and more than that, Gertrude had used Zackery, instead of the preferred Zack.

Father's voice quickly spoke to us, "Boys—over here," and we went back to join the family.

Zackery was so cross that his face was red. I didn't feel so great myself, being embarrassed like that right out in front of everyone, but I said nothing.

Zack didn't say anything either, but I knew that he'd like to say plenty, with most of it directed at Gertrude.

As soon as we had finished our eating and Father had another drink from the water dish, we headed back, single file, toward our nest. As usual, Hiram brought up the rear. He never seemed in a hurry to go anywhere. Yet he was an easy-going friendly fellow and didn't seem to get into trouble as he loitered along behind. I often wondered why Father and Mother didn't just leave him alone and let him take his own time. But they didn't. One or the other of them always seemed to linger at the back of the line and made sure that Hiram was closely following the rest of the family and was never completely on his own.

That night, after we had all been bedded down, I couldn't sleep. There were so many things that I didn't know or understand. I decided to have a little talk with Mother. I squeezed out from under her wing and moved up beside her.

She turned and looked at me and caressed me gently with her beak. I wished that she wouldn't do that. It made me feel like a little child again. I looked around to see if anybody had been watching. There was no one. I was relieved, but I pulled back from Mother and I think that she understood that I hadn't liked her caress.

"I can't sleep." I complained.

"Want to talk?" she asked.

Now, how does she know that, I wondered but I didn't ask.

"We met a guy today," I said in what I hoped was an off-hand manner.

"I noticed," said Mother.

"His name's Clinton," I went on.

"We know his family," said Mother.

"Are they—are they—a nice family?" I asked her, hoping that she wouldn't object to us knowing Clinton.

"A fine family—though I think that Clinton might be just a little headstrong. They worry about him."

I thought of Clinton and his determination to visit the other pond on his own. I wondered if Mother had overheard our conversation but she didn't say any more.

"Why do you say that?" I asked, after waiting for a few minutes.

"I've been watching. His Mother and Father have trouble keeping him in line and she has confided in me that they are concerned."

"It's not wrong to want to learn about things, is it?" My annoyance and impatience showed in my voice in spite of my effort to keep it out.

"Oh, no," said Mother hastily. "It's not wrong at all to be curious about life and all that is around us. We just need to be cautious, that's all. We need to learn to accept advice and direction from someone else who has been around longer than we have, and to listen to their judgment on some things. Your father is very wise and has lived for a number of years. When he advises against a venture, you would be wise to listen."

I didn't say anything for a moment. I hated to argue with Mother but I did think that she was going a bit too far. It seemed perfectly safe about the farm and the pond. I still hadn't seen anything that looked like an enemy and neither had Zack, and we both had our eyes and ears open. I thought that perhaps both Father and Mother were a bit too cautious with age. Were all old folks like that?

"You're in too big a hurry, Quackery," Mother went on. "You will be given much more freedom as time goes on. Believe me. We'll know when you are ready to be on your own."

"And in the meantime," I said, in an irritated voice, "we can't even talk to anyone."

"We want to be sure that you associate with the right—"

I interrupted, though I had been taught not to do so, "And how will we know who are the right—?"

But Mother cut me short.

"Don't be sassy, Quackery," she said. "I'm more than willing to discuss anything that you'd like to discuss, but I am your mother and I won't tolerate rudeness."

"I'm sorry," I apologized. And I was sorry—sort of.

"First of all," Mother went on, speaking as though nothing had happened in our conversation to interrupt our discussion, "your father and I will try to show you by our associations who we feel would be good friends for you."

"You mean, our own kind?"

"Not necessarily. There are many fine families in the barn-yard besides our own kind. And some of our own kind, unfortunately, don't have good reputations. So it isn't which family you are from, but how one behaves, that is important."

"Who are we Mother?" I asked suddenly.

"What do you mean?" Mother prompted in surprise.

"I mean, who are we? What is our kind?"

"Well, we are ducks," she said and I knew from her tone that she had expected me to know that.

"And what about Clinton?" I asked.

"He's a duck, too."

"And the other ones?"

"Which other ones?"

"The ones on the pond. The big white ones who talk funny."

Mother smiled. "Those are geese," she said. "They are fine folk too. And they don't talk 'funny.' They just talk louder and much more than we do. You can understand them if you listen closely. Some of them are close friends of your father and me."

"How come the others don't go to the pond every day?"

"Which others?"

"Well, those great big ones, who are always strutting around the yard puffing and pushing. The ones that Prudence is afraid of."

"The turkeys? I don't know. It seems that they just don't care for swimming."

I thought the turkeys very strange indeed if they didn't like to swim and was about to strike them from my list of possible future friends when Mother spoke again.

"They are different from us, that's true, but Mrs. Strutt is a most friendly person. Her husband seems a bit gruff, but I think that he is a fine man as well."

So, mother hadn't struck the turkey family off her list just because they were different. I wondered about that.

"None of those other ones have been at the pond either," I reminded Mother.

"The chickens? No. They don't seem to be swimmers either."

"Don't their mothers and fathers teach them? I asked, wondering about the lack in their education.

Mother smiled again. "I'm not sure that their mothers and fathers know how," she said simply.

I was about to ask how they could be so dumb, when mother spoke again. "And, now young man," she said, "You'd better get back to bed. It's getting late and you should be sleeping. Tomorrow will be another big day."

I wanted to protest and ask more questions but I knew that Mother expected to be obeyed and so I told her good night and pushed back under her wing.

It was still hard to go to sleep. There were so many things to think about. So many things to learn. It seemed that I was the only one who ever asked questions. Even Zack didn't bother asking. He planned to find the answers for all of his questions on his own. Maybe Zack was right. I didn't know. Maybe one shouldn't bother asking but should just look for the answers. Maybe one should just be free to choose his own friends and take the consequences if he made wrong choices. I didn't see how much harm could come to one by doing that.

Chapter Six

Zackery

Each day we were given a bit more freedom, though I was still conscious of Father's and Mother's eyes upon me. I was conscious of another thing, too. As we took less care and supervision each day, Father and Mother were free to give more of their attention to our neighbors. It seemed to me that Mother must have been missing the contact with others while confined to our constant care. Now she seemed to take great pleasure in chatting briefly with the other mothers of the farmyard as we walked to and from the pond or gathered for the grain that was scattered for us.

I had wondered where the grain came from. Each morning it was there, and by the end of the day as we left after our final feeding, it was all gone. Yet somehow, by some miracle, it was there when we needed it again the next morning.

I asked Mother about it.

"The farmer's wife scatters it," said Mother in answer to my question.

"The farmer's wife?"

"Yes. The farmer and his wife own the farm, the pond—and each one of us as well."

"They own *us*?"

"That's right."

That puzzled me. How could they own us? I hadn't even seen them. If they owned us why weren't we under their rule?

"If they own us," I said to Mother, "why don't they control us? I mean—I haven't seen them around telling us when we can go to the pond or when we can eat or anything."

"Oh, no," said Mother. "They give us freedom to make all of those choices."

"Then what does it mean, to own us?" I persisted.

Mother thought very carefully for several minutes. Then she said slowly, "I guess that to own us means a promise to care for us. It seems that they ask nothing of us really, but they do take special care of us. Yet they would be completely within their rights to ask anything of us that they wished. Instead, they provide our food, our pond and our nest. Yes, I guess that owning us means that they have decided to take good care of us."

It seemed strange to me but I was willing to accept the care of our owners. Still, it did seem awfully one-sided.

"Don't we do anything—well—sort of—in return?" I asked Mother.

"Well, yes. Of course we do. The roosters crow. They are the guards of the farmyard. I don't think that anyone ever told them that it is their job and they must do it. They just assumed that duty as theirs because they do it best. They have wonderfully loud voices and they can sound the alarm whenever it is needed."

I thought of the roosters. I knew that what Mother said was true, though I had not as yet heard the roosters sound an alarm. I had heard them give the early morning wake-up call, though. It always rang out clearly across the farmyard.

"What about the geese?" I asked Mother.

"The geese are wonderful about keeping the orchard and garden clean," said Mother. "Not only do they eat the bugs and insects that do damage, but they eat the weeds as well."

"And the hens?"

"The hens lay eggs every day. Haven't you seen the farmer's boy walk by with a basket brimming with eggs? Those are from the hens and what the farmer's family doesn't use, the farmer's wife sells in town."

We were interrupted then by Zack.

"Quackery," he said, "there's really good picking over here."

I hadn't even finished asking Mother all of my questions yet. I had wanted to know what our special service to the farmer and his family was, but I had an idea that Zack had something on his mind besides the plentiful grain on the ground and so I followed him.

As soon as we were out of earshot, Zack pulled me aside and whispered, "Remember what Clinton said about the big pond?"

"You mean the one across the road?"

"Right. Well some of the chickens are saying that there is to be a real big wind today. Clinton says that it would be a great day to try the pond. How about it?"

"I don't know," I hesitated. "I'm not sure that Mother would—"

But Zackery cut me short. "Mother needn't know. She is busy visiting more now and we could sneak off without her even seeing us."

"Father might—" I began, but Zack stopped me on that, too.

"Father's way over there," he said, nodding his head at the far corner of the yard where Father was feeding and chatting with some of the other men-folk.

"I don't think we should," I said reluctantly.

"Then you don't want to come?"

"Well, I want to, but I don't think that we should."

"Okay, you big sissy, stay here if you want to. Miss all the fun. I don't care. I'm going with Clinton."

I cast my eyes around hoping that Gertrude might be somewhere nearby to tattle on us again. She wasn't. I knew that Zack shouldn't go but I wasn't about to tell on him and make him mad at me, and have the other fellows all thinking that I was a tattletale.

"You coming?" asked Clinton.

Zack looked at me. I did not move.

"Well, I am," he answered Clinton, "but I don't think Quack here is."

"What's wrong," said Clinton. "You a mama's boy?"

He said it in a sing-songy way and they both laughed at me and moved off. I watched them as they were joined by Godfrey Goose, the special friend of Clinton's. I didn't much care for the looks of Godfrey. He was big and arrogant and when he waddled he did it with an exaggerated swagger.

I could hear them laughing as they went and I knew that

they were laughing at me. "Mama's boy," they had called me. I didn't want to be a mama's boy. At least I sure didn't want the other fellows thinking of me in that way.

I moved slowly toward my father. He was doing more chatting than eating. He was talking to Mr. Whitehall, the big gander, and to Mr. Lucky of another duck family.

"When did they see him?" I heard Father ask.

"Yesterday," was the answer. "He was in very close to the barn."

"I guess we all need to be extra careful," said Father. "He will be back again for sure."

Even as Father spoke I saw him look about the farmyard and begin to look for his family. Mother was there. Father's eyes went to her first and then he began to look for each of the children.

Hiram and Hazel were over near the fence. Hazel was laying in the sun with her head tucked under one wing. Gertrude and Fluff were chatting. I could hear them giggle every now and then. Prudence, who was always shy and hesitant, stayed close to Mother, and Oscar, who was always boastful because of his size, was busy strutting around for the benefit of the youth of the farmyard.

Father kept on looking. I knew without looking up that he was about to ask me the dreaded question. I tried to move away, but I wasn't fast enough.

"Where's Zackery?" he asked me.

I was caught. I looked up and my eyes traveled around the yard as though I too was looking. I didn't know how to answer Father. I knew that Zack would never forgive me if I told on him, yet how could I tell a lie?

"Zack?" I said lamely, in an effort to conceal what I knew.

"Mr. Whitehall says that a hawk has been seen hanging around."

"Is—is—a hawk dangerous?" I stammered. I had never met a hawk before.

"Extremely dangerous," said Father. "Especially to the young. He can snatch a youngster before they even know what his shadow means."

I felt nervous then. What if something happened to Zack? I was about to tell all I knew to Father but before I could say anything, he moved abruptly away. He went to talk with Mother, concern showing in his face.

They soon gathered all of us together and headed us to the pond. It was clear that they felt safer where they would have the protection of a dive if the hawk should appear again. I could tell that they were worried about Zack. I was worried, too. I did wish that he would hurry back.

The wind did begin to blow. It made waves on the pond. At first, they were gentle and I loved the feeling of being lifted slightly and then swished down. As the afternoon progressed, the wind became stronger and stronger. I still loved the feeling. It was like a thrill ride. Up and down, up and down, we rode the waves.

Prudence began to complain. It was scary, she said. Mother assured her that there was no way that she could be hurt by the rising and falling water, and to just let herself go and enjoy the feel of it, but Prudence claimed that she couldn't enjoy it. It made her tummy feel sick. I thought that she was just being silly.

I knew that Mother and Father were both still worried about Zack, I heard them ask the other family members if they had seen Zackery leave the yard. They all said that they hadn't. Gertrude had to add her piece about Zackery hanging out with the wrong crowd and asking for trouble. Mother made no comment but the troubled look in her eyes increased.

It was mid-afternoon before I noticed Zack swimming toward us. He dove for the last distance and came to the surface again right in the midst of the family. I knew that he hoped that Father and Mother hadn't even noticed that he had been missing and that he could just sneak back in without the family noticing. It didn't work. As soon as he surfaced, Father was beside him.

"Where have you been?" Father asked.

Zackery gave me an 'if-you-dared' look. Then he looked back at Father.

I knew that he wanted to say that he had been right there all of the time. I also knew that he could tell by Father's face that it would be silly to say that. Father knew that he had not been there.

"I got separated, I guess," said Zack. "I didn't see you leave the farmyard. I went back to the nest but you weren't there, so I came over here."

Father looked doubtful. I didn't think that he really believed Zack but he didn't say that he didn't. Instead he said, "Well, you were separated for an awfully long time. I would suggest that in future you pay more attention to what you are doing—and to what the rest of the family is doing. There is a hawk hanging around. It's extremely dangerous, and I want you to have the protection of the family and the pond. You stay with the family from now on."

"Yes sir," said Zack reluctantly, and yet with relief.

It had worked. He had gotten away with it. It made me wonder if he'd be smart enough to leave well enough alone, or if he'd try it again.

Chapter Seven

The Storm

"You should have been with us," Zack whispered to me later that night when we were tucked under Mother's wings and were supposed to be sleeping. "I've never had so much fun in my life."

"We had waves here, too," I said stubbornly.

"Nothing like we had. Boy, was it fun. I can hardly wait for another wind."

"You're not going again, are you?" I asked, incredulously. "You heard what Father said."

"A hawk," said Zack. "He'd keep me here, missing out on all the fun, just because of a hawk."

"Hawks are dangerous. They like baby ducks."

"Well, I'm not a baby duck," declared Zack hotly. "Hadn't you noticed? I'm not a kid anymore, Quack, and I'm not tied to Mama like you are either. I want to have some fun in life. I'm not going to sit around here tied to the folds just . . . "

"You're taking chances, can't you see that?" I argued. "You're liable to get in farther than you can handle if you don't watch out."

"Oh, phooey," said Zack. "You sit around and be Mama's

good little boy if you want to. Me, I'm going to have some fun out of life."

I wanted to have fun, too. Yet I wasn't about to disobey the advice and orders of my parents in order to do it. What if they did know what they were talking about?

"Mother," came a whiney, shrill voice," I can't sleep. Zackery and Quackery won't quit talking."

It was Gertrude. Mother poked her head under her wing and said, "Shh-hh," and we did.

"Someday I'm gonna smack her," grumbled Zack. I thought that Gertrude might well have it coming, but I did hope that Zack didn't carry through with his threat.

The next morning was a clear, bright day and we all followed Father and Mother to the farmyard for our breakfast of grain before we left for the pond.

Clinton was there, strutting around, big and self-important.

He sauntered toward Zack and me, and I wanted to move out of there. I was afraid to, for fear they would start calling me names again.

"Did you get caught?" whispered Clinton.

Zack grinned. I thought that he was even more proud of himself because he did get caught and yet was willing to risk this foolish stunt again.

"Yeah," he said a bit boastfully. "Did you?"

"Naw," said Clinton. "They didn't even miss me."

I wondered if that was the truth or another lie.

"Is it going to blow today?" asked Zack, to show Clinton that he was ready to go again.

"Don't know. I'll ask Godfrey."

Clinton was soon back, Godfrey swaggering along beside him. Godfrey studied the sky and said with assurance, "Ain't no use going today. Waves won't be worth nothin'."

I was relieved. At least I wouldn't need to worry about Zack for another day.

"Might find something else to do," suggested Godfrey, and

my heart began to pound again.

"Like what?" asked Zack.

"Don't know, off-hand," said Godfrey with a boastful grin, "but I can usually come up with something."

I was about to make a comment when Father called to us. Zack looked thoroughly disgusted but he followed me to see what Father wanted.

"We're ready to go to the pond," Father said, and we knew that he meant that we were to follow without question. Zackery asked one anyway.

"How come we're going so early?"

"There's a storm moving in. We want to get our swimming and feeding done before it gets here."

I gave Zack a look that said, "See? Big shot Godfrey didn't know what he was talking about after all." Zack looked up at the clear sky overhead and looked back at me with, "We'll see. I don't see any storm."

It was calm on the pond when we first entered the water. I kept thinking of the fun waves the day before and hoped that the wind would blow again. I also thought of Zack and his fun on the open pond. It must have been a great deal more fun to rock up and down on the higher waves. I sure would like to try it.

About mid-morning, the sky began to darken and the wind came up. Large clouds rolled in quickly from nowhere. I couldn't believe how quickly it had changed. Then the rain came. The rain did not bother us. It rolled gently from our backs and joined the waters of the pond. But with the rain, it seemed that the food became more scarce and after searching unprofitably for a time, Father suggested that we return to the farmyard where dinner would be waiting for us.

The wind and rain increased. Mother led us back to our nest and all snuggled in. It had been a cold rain and we all felt a bit chilled and welcomed the thought of warming under Mother's feathery body. I think that even Zack welcomed it, though he tried to look tough.

We had just settled down nicely and began to warm some when I felt my feet getting wet. I shifted my position, hoping to at least keep my body dry. It wasn't any use. The water was coming in quickly and there was no way that one could move to escape it.

It was Gertrude who called the alarm.

"Mother," she said in her shrill voice, "the water's pouring in and we are all getting wet."

Mother checked the nest. Gertrude was right. Prudence began to whimper.

"What will we do now? We have no place to go," she cried.

"Shh-hh," said Mother. "Of course we have somewhere to go. "We'll just move over to one of the farm buildings. They are all warm and dry."

So Mother led us to one of the buildings on the farm and Father followed at the end of the line to hasten up the stragglers, which were Hiram and Hazel.

We were soon tucked into a nest, newly scratched out of the straw. It was warm and dry there, just as Mother had said it would be, and we settled down to warm up and dry off.

The wind increased. I thought again of Godfrey and his boast about being able to predict the weather. He had sure missed it today. I smiled to myself. Maybe Zack would learn that his new friend wasn't so smart after all.

We were just settling down to sleep when there was a strong gust of wind and a strange, creak and groan from the building. Then before we could even move, there was a tumbling and grinding as the boards tore from one another and the little barn began to fall around us.

"Quick," screamed Mother. "Jump! Jump!"

We were quick to obey. Mother, with wings flapping and voice crying, led the way, Father right behind her. We scurried after. There was one last sickening groan as the building came tumbling down and then all was quiet except for the sound of

the wind and rain.

Father at once began to search us out and check us. "Gertrude, Prudence, are you all right?" Prudence was crying, but they both seemed unharmed. "Oscar, Boyd, Hiram?" Yes, they were fine. "Zackery? Quackery?" We were okay. "Hazel, Fluff?" Hazel answered but Fluff did not. Father looked around us. Fluff was not there. Mother began to dash about, calling loudly. There was no Fluff. All of us were concerned now. Where was Fluff? Had she been unable to clear the building before it fell? It seemed so, but I could imagine someone being trapped in that pile of rubble.

We all dashed around excitedly. What could we do? We called to her and then listened, but we did not hear her answer.

Mother was sick with worry.

The big farm dog drew near. He had heard all of the commotion. We didn't care much for the farm dog. He was always running through the feeding area and sending geese, chickens, turkeys and us scurrying with flapping wings in an effort to get out of his way. He never seemed to hurt anyone. He just scared us all half out of our wits. He seemed to take great pleasure in it, and I always ate with one eye watching out for him so that I might move quickly if need be.

He came fast now, running as usual, and we all flapped our wings and squawked our way out of his pathway. He began to bark and dig at the fallen pile of building. Mother began to scream at him that his careless digging might hurt her baby further, but he paid no attention to her.

We were all screaming now, calling out to the dog to be careful, that one of our family was still there somewhere in the pile. Our panic grew.

The noise brought the farmer. He looked at us and at the dog. Then he called the dog and made him lie down in the wet grass beside the fallen building, and then carefully, oh so carefully, he began to lift the fallen boards and lay them aside. We were about to give up, thinking that Fluff could not have

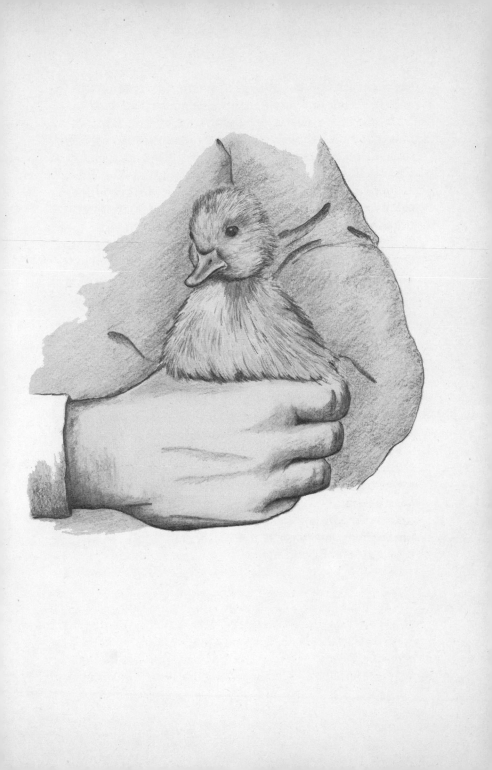

possibly survived the collapse, when the farmer lifted a board and there beneath it, secured in a little pocket that had formed from one board resting on another, was Fluff. She did not move, and for an awful second I thought that she was dead. But then she blinked at the light and shook her head at the rain that began to fall upon her, and rose unsteadily to her feet.

"Well, I'll be," said the farmer, reaching down and lifting her gently out. "You're okay. You were a mighty lucky girl."

He placed Fluff on the ground beside Mother and spoke again. "Is this what all of the fuss was about? Well, she's okay. One, two, three, four, five, six, seven, eight, and now nine. They're all here. All okay. Now you'd better take them all into the barn and out of the rain. You'll be safe there; and he drove us toward the barn.

Father showed us how to do the man's bidding and we were soon out of the rain, rejoicing over all being safe together.

Mother crooned over and over to Fluff. I think that Fluff was quite pleased with all of the attention. I was certainly relieved to see Fluff. Oh, I know that she was a nuisance at times, when she wanted to tag along after me, but I would have missed her terribly if anything had happened to her.

I thought of the farm dog, too. I hadn't cared much for the fellow, but if it hadn't been for his barking, the farmer would not have come to our rescue. Maybe he was good for something after all.

Then I cuddled up closely to my family under the warmth of our mother's downy wings and felt very thankful that each one of us was safe. Even Gertrude.

Chapter Eight

Danger

When we awoke the next morning, the wind and rain had stopped. We went back to the farmyard where we found that the storm had done a great deal of damage. Not only was the small building where we had sought shelter scattered in a pile of broken boards, but limbs were torn from trees, and, down along the pasture fence, one large tree had been completely uprooted and left lying broken and smashed on the ground.

There was no grain when we went to the yard. We all stood around hungrily and some of the more vocal inhabitants were quite noisy about the fact that it was morning and they were hungry. We were about ready to give up and head for the pond when the boy who gathered eggs came to the farmyard with the morning feed. The farmer's wife was nowhere in sight. The boy tossed out the food, making big circles with his arms as he did so.

"I've got a new sister," he called as he fed us. "I've wanted a sister for a long, long time."

I thought about my sisters. Especially of Fluff, whose life I had feared for the night before. I would have hated so to lose her. I liked each one of my sisters just fine and would have really missed them if something had happened to any one of them. Still, I couldn't understand how the boy was so excited over getting just one.

Feeding was rather difficult that morning. It was wet all around the farmyard. The chickens and turkeys seemed to just hate it. They walked around every puddle instead of through it. They didn't seem to think that water was good for anything, except to drink. I found myself wishing that they would try it. They might find it fun.

We went to the pond as soon as we had finished breakfast. It was a calm morning after the storm. The feeding was good and I was thoroughly enjoying myself eating and diving. I loved the water. I loved the feeling of strength in my feet as I pushed myself forward and then down, down, down. *I'm getting to be a pretty strong swimmer* I was thinking, very proud of myself, when there was a swish beside me and Oscar went sliding by in an effortless fashion.

"Have you a race," he challenged, and I knew that he knew very well that there wasn't any hope that I might keep up with him.

I swam off by myself, rather miffed that Oscar had spoiled my high opinion of myself.

I was swimming along, wallowing in ruffled feathers, when there was a sharp cry from my Mother, and splashes all around me. I took a moment to look instead of doing as Father and Mother had drilled us. We had been taught to dive immediately when the alarm sounded, without a moment's hesitation. The brief look upward was almost my undoing, for there, above my head and swooping down at an alarming rate of speed, was the hawk. I knew instinctively that it was him. He looked so fast, so powerful, so frightening, and I ducked under the water just as I heard the splash of his wings as they hit the water above me before he pulled out of his dive and climbed back into the sky.

It was a terrible experience. My heart was pounding. My head spinning. I stayed under the water for as long as I could, not knowing if I dared to ever surface again. At last my lungs could stand it no longer, and I arose from the water's depths, looking nervously about.

Father, Mother and the family were swimming some distance from me and with panic still clutching at me, I swam to join them.

Just as I drew near to the family there was a cry of, "Dive!" from Father, and a shadow passed over my head. I knew without looking up that it was the hawk again and I did not wait for a second signal, but dived immediately. Again I heard the swish above me.

This time as I swam under the water I made an effort to stay near the family. We stayed under for as long as we could and then surfaced again. Father kept a sharp eye out and soon commanded us to dive again. It was a terrible feeling, knowing that the hawk circled in the sky above us, ready to drop down the moment that we made an appearance.

We swam, then dived, re-surfaced, and swam, then dived again. I noticed that each time that we resurfaced we were closer to the reeds that grew along one side of the pond. Father was carefully steering us in that direction. At last we reached them. There was a measure of security in the reeds, though we were all still nervous and Father and Mother kept an eye on the sky.

It was several moments until my heart was beating at a

normal rate. I knew that the others were just as frightened as I. We all knew that had we been on the ground instead of in the water, things would have been much different. In the water, we were mobile and could dive and hide for many minutes at a time. On land, we were slow and somewhat awkward. Unless we had found something under which to hide very quickly, one or two of us most surely would have been missing. I was thankful for the wisdom of our father and mother. They knew where our protection lay.

It was getting late in the day. In fact, the sun was setting in the western sky before Father decided that it was safe for us to leave the pond. We walked slowly, single file. I noticed my brothers and sisters, like myself, still watched the sky as we walked, but the hawk did not appear.

I was hungry when I reached the farmyard. We had been too busy and too frightened while at the pond to feed well, and it had been a long day. I ate hungrily now. I didn't even look around for Clinton or Godfrey. I didn't even think to watch for the farm dog until there was the sound of running, and chickens squawked, turkeys gobbled, geese honked and ducks quacked, as all of us, with a great flapping of our wings, tried to get out of the way.

I almost didn't make it. I was too busy eating and hadn't noticed the dog until it was almost too late. One of his speeding legs caught my outspread wing and spun me around, sending me reeling into a fence post. I lay there, stunned for a moment. Then I struggled back to my feet and shook my head, trying to gain my senses. Sometimes it was awfully hard to remember that I should feel grateful to that dog.

I knew that he would likely be back, so I fed near the fence instead of in the middle of the yard. I didn't want to be hit again.

He did come back, too, running just as fast as before and scattering all of the fowl as he dashed, barking, through our midst. Mr. Strutters, the large turkey gobbler, complained loudly. The dog was most inconsiderate, he said, and something should be done about him. He didn't say what should be done, or who should do it. Several of the other fowl agreed with Mr. Strutters, but they didn't come up with any suggestions either. I went back to feeding, still staying close to the fence. The grain was not plentiful there and it took a great deal more scratching and looking but I did feel safer.

The farm wife was still not seen around the farmyard. I guessed that, like mother, the care and the training of the new baby, kept her too busy for visiting. The boy still scattered the grain morning and evening. We really didn't care who brought it, as long as it was there for the eating.

We had not returned to our nest after the bad rainstorm. I don't know if it dried out again or not, but I don't think that it would have had the same comfort as before. Besides, we were getting much bigger now. We couldn't all fit under Mother at the same time. Some of us liked to be more on our own, and snuggled down close to Mother and Father, but not under her wings anymore. Prudence still chose to crawl beneath Mother's protective wing and she was sometimes joined by the other girls. Even Boyd, when he thought that no one was looking, would sneak under on occasion.

Zack would have never showed his need, or desire, for protection. He felt much too big for that. In fact, he didn't even like to sleep close to the rest of us. He always lay down just a little ways away. I noticed that the distance got just a little further away night by night. Father would speak to him now and then and bring him back closer to the family. I knew that Zack resented it. It was very important to Zack to feel grown-up and on his own.

"Look at me," he said to me one day, "almost all feathered out and still being treated like a child."

"Oscar's even bigger than you, and more feathered-out too, and he doesn't mind being treated like a—a—," I didn't want to say 'child.' It made all of us seem young. Zack cut in, "Well,

Oscar's a big sissy. Look at him. Great big, overgrown, sissy."

Zack never could forgive Oscar for being naturally bigger and stronger than he.

"Well, I don't plan to sit around being told what to do all of my life."

"What about today?" I reminded him. "And the hawk?"

"Hawk? Phooey! I could have done anything on my own that we did out there. All you need to do is watch for him and then dive."

I was worried about Zack.

"You're not going to try anything silly again are you?" I asked anxiously.

"Silly? Like what?"

"I don't know. Like going to the big pond across the road?"

"Sure, I'm going to the big pond across the road. Just as soon as a good wind comes up."

"It's dangerous . . . " I started to say but Zack stopped me.

"How do you know it's dangerous? You been there? No. Of course not. I hate it when folks keep telling you how dangerous something is when they haven't even tried it themselves."

"But Mother says . . . " I began again.

"Has she been there? No, nor Father either. That's stupid. They don't even know if it's dangerous or not. Why don't you go and see for yourself?"

I shook my head.

"It's just good fun," went on Zack. "Nothing dangerous about it at all. I don't think that big folks want us to have fun."

"That's not it," I argued. "They just don't want us to get hurt, that's all."

"That's the story they feed us, but I don't believe them," persisted Zack.

I knew that there was no use arguing further. Zack was not going to listen to me. I tucked my head under my growing wing and shut my eyes, pretending to be asleep.

Chapter Nine

Attack

"There's a storm coming," Zack whispered in my ear the next day. "You want to come with us?"

I started to shake my head when a voice behind Zack sung out, "Mama's boy still wants to stay close to Mama."

It was Clinton. It made me angry and I wished that I could reach out and peck him a good one.

Godfrey was there, too. I had wanted to argue with Zack, to try to reason with him about the dangers of letting those two witless fellows drag him off to the pond with them, but when I saw that the other two fellows were right there with him, I knew that it was no use. I ignored them and turned and waddled away.

Father soon gave the signal for us to head for the pond and I followed him without looking back. I knew that Zack would probably hide himself until we left and then leave the yard to go to the big pond across the road.

The day went slowly for me. The storm came and the wind made the waves carry us up in the air and then drop us with a swish. It was great fun and Oscar and I tried to find the highest waves to ride. Fluff joined us. She was still smaller than the rest of us, and she looked like she was getting a better ride than anyone else. Her waves always looked higher, but I reminded myself that it might be because she was smaller than us, in comparison.

It was great fun riding the waves. We still hadn't forgotten about the hawk and we saw Father and Mother carefully watching the sky and we knew that they hadn't forgotten about the hawk either. If, in our fun, we would stray too far from them, they would quickly call us back.

I thought often of Zack. He would be having lots of fun. The waves in the bigger, more open pond, would be much bigger than our waves here. I also thought of the danger. I knew that Father and Mother feared crossing the road. I didn't know what the danger was, having never seen the road and what went on there, but I knew that they thought that the danger of crossing was too great to risk anything that might be found on the other side.

I thought of the hawk, too. If Zack and Clinton and Godfrey were busy riding the waves, who would be on lookout for the hawk?

It bothered me. Father had not asked me this time about Zack but I knew that he missed him. I saw him look around the pond often, and I knew that he was checking to see if Zack might be with some of the other duck families.

Zack did not appear and the day went slowly by.

We had left the pond and were feeding in the yard before I saw Zack again. He grinned at me. I knew that he was telling me that I had missed a great time. He would be anxious to tell me all about it. I moved in the opposite direction as I fed. I didn't want to hear about it, at least not yet.

But I couldn't avoid Zack for long. He was soon by my side.

"Boy did we have fun. You should have seen those waves."

"Yeah," I said, "we had some nice ones, too."

"Those little things? You don't even know what a big wave is. You should have been with us."

I just looked at him and said nothing.

"See," went on Zack, "I've been to the pond, crossed the road, coming and going, and do I look like I came to any harm?"

"Well, no but . . ."

"You see, it's all just scare stories. Somebody tells it to somebody else, and then they add something to it and tell it to somebody else. And so it goes, on and on. I tell you Quack, it's as safe crossing that road as it is walking right here in this farmyard."

I thought of the farm dog rushing through and was about to agree with Zack. Sometimes I didn't feel too safe right where I was.

Then I thought of the hawk. Zack must have read my mind.

"We take turns watching for the hawk. He never even showed. We can care for ourselves. We're almost full grown now."

Zack was getting pretty big, but he did have a ways to go yet to catch Father. I said nothing, but went on eating. About that time the dog came slamming through the flock again, scattering everyone in any direction that they could flee from his running feet and barking mouth. I ducked under the fence and Zack was right beside me.

"Someday . . . " he muttered, but he didn't finish it.

Zack wandered off to join Clinton and Godfrey then, and I went on with my eating, but I couldn't forget what Zack had said. *Maybe it is just scare stories. Maybe there is nothing to fear in crossing the road. Maybe our parents are too protective. I sure would like to try out the high waves on the other pond. It might be okay to try it just once. Like Zack said, we could all take turns watching for the hawk.* I'd do some thinking about it.

It seemed that we had just settled ourselves for the night when there was a loud clucking and squawking from the chicken house. At first I thought that it might just be a family squabble of some kind and was about to tuck my head back under my wing, when Father spoke.

"Keep a lookout," he said. "There must be trouble about for them to be so upset."

Mother moved about nervously. She, too, feared that there was danger about.

I could hear the turkeys talking it over in loud, excited voices. They, too, felt that the roosters and hens must have good reason for the general alarm. All eyes probed the darkness but we could see nothing.

I moved in closer to Father and Mother like I was told. The other family members did likewise, except for Zack. I could see him lying by himself a short distance away and he was looking into the darkness. When he saw no movement there, he tucked his head back under his wing and disregarded Father's signal.

Father called his name, but Zack chose not to hear.

The noise from the chickens quieted down and we began to feel that perhaps the danger, whatever it had been, had passed. We settled down again. I was just dropping off to sleep when there was a loud honking from the geese. We all stirred again. It was clear that something was amiss.

"Maybe we should head for the barn?" Father said to Mother. She agreed, her nervousness showing plainly, and began to round up the family. Zack still did not move.

We had just begun to move off in the direction of the barn when there was a shadowy movement to our right and then a quick forward leap, and Zack let out a tortured scream of fright and pain. Some creature in the darkness had crept up and seized him.

What a clatter there was then. You could not hear yourself think for the awful racket. Everyone was screaming and crying and Zack was yelling, "Save me, save me," at the top of his voice, but there was really nothing that any of us could do.

It was the farm dog who came to our rescue again. Almost

the instant that the strange creature had grabbed Zack, the farm dog was there, his deep bass voice booming out a warning, his fangs bared and his teeth ready. The creature dropped Zack and fled into the darkness of the night.

The father and the boy both came out, a lantern lighting up the otherwise dark farmyard. They checked out the hen house and the yard. It was the boy who found poor Zack. He could barely move and the ragged teeth marks of the animal were bleeding from his back. The boy picked him up and held him out to the man.

"It got one of the ducks," he said. "No wonder they are all so scared."

"We'd better put them all in the barn tonight and shut the door," said the farmer.

"What do you think it was?" asked the boy.

"Likely a coyote. They've been coming in pretty close lately."

It was a long time before the racket subsided. With a great deal of honking, clucking, gobbling, and quacking, we were all secured for the night behind closed doors. It was some time before we were able to settle down. We were all still nervous and the least little stirring would set someone off again.

Zack laid next to Mother. I knew that he was in great pain. The farmer had put something on his wounds and that seemed to be all that could be done for him. I wanted to say something to try and comfort him but there didn't seem to be anything to say. I noticed that he stayed very close to the family now. I wondered how long he would be with us, or if as soon as his wounds healed he would insist on being on his own again. At least he would have another chance. It might have been different. Zack could have easily been carried off by the animal and become his breakfast. I shuddered at the thought. I guess we all had been really lucky. We had another reason for being thankful to the farm dog.

Chapter Ten

The Big Pond

Zack healed slowly. His wounds did keep him from crossing the road to the big pond, and his friends dropped by to wish him a speedy recovery. I think that they were missing him in their daring adventures. They told him that they had been to the pond again and that it had been great fun. Zack looked very sorrowful. He was missing out on a lot of fun because of his injury.

He swam with the family and obeyed the orders of Father and Mother. He didn't even stray too far away at night—at first. Gradually he began to sleep further away again and to swim out further from the family during the day as well. I knew that he was getting better, and I knew that he really hadn't changed.

It wasn't long until I could tell that he felt ready to go to the big pond again. I could see him watching the sky and I knew that he was waiting for a windy day.

As we fed in the farmyard one morning, Zack walked over close to me.

"Notice the wind?" he asked me.

I nodded that I had.

"We should have the biggest waves ever on the pond today," Zack said. "I can hardly wait."

"Are you sure that your back is okay?"

"Fine," boasted Zack. "It's almost healed."

I looked at his back. You could still see the teeth marks but Zack was right. It was almost healed.

"How about coming?" asked Zack. "You'll have the time of your life."

"I don't know," I hesitated. *Boy, I would love to try it,* I thought.

"Father and Mother don't watch us as closely anymore," Zack went on. "Bet they wouldn't even notice that you were gone."

I knew that what Zack said was true. Father and Mother were giving us more freedom. Still, I knew that they didn't want, nor expect, us to cross the road.

"We'll watch out for you," went on Zack. "The other fellows have been there a dozen times. They know all about what to watch for."

"I don't know," I still said.

Clinton swaggered over. He was followed closely by Godfrey.

"Ready Zack?" said Clinton.

"Sure," said Zack. "Okay if I bring my brother?"

"The mama's boy?" said Godfrey with a sneer. "Isn't he afraid to cross the road without mama there to hold his hand?"

"He's not afraid," said Zack, surprising me with his defense. "Are you, Quack?"

I pulled myself to my full height. Of course I was not afraid. It was just dumb to take chances, that was all.

"C'mon Zack," said Clinton.

"C'mon Quack," said Zack, and I found myself moving along behind them,

My good sense told me that I was doing wrong. I shouldn't be taking this foolish risk just because the other fellows did. I shouldn't be following them just because they called me names and teased me. I shouldn't need to prove that I was just as fearless as they were. The whole thing didn't make sense, yet, here I was, following them as though I had no head on my shoulders to do my own thinking.

Well, I do want to try out the pond. Maybe it isn't so dangerous after all. It won't hurt just to try it once, will it?

We reached the road and I looked at the strange, long, smooth area. It stretched as far as one could see toward the east and as far as one could see toward the west. It was wide. As I looked across it I wondered how long it would take a slow-moving duck to walk across. I wished that I could fly, but my wings were too stubby to lift me up.

There were moving things on the road. The first one that swished by scared me half to death. I had thought that the running dog moved quickly, but it was nothing in comparison to these things. With a whish and a roar they would appear from nowhere and be gone just as quickly in the other direction.

Clinton swaggered up beside me. "Nothing to it," he boasted. "You just watch for an opening and then run for it."

It sounded simple enough but I wondered as I watched the big engines flash on by just how simple it would really be.

"I'll go first," said Godfrey.

He waited for a break in the traffic and then, with a flutter and a leap, he was out on the road and flapping his way quickly across. Just as he cleared the other side another big machine went flashing by. I held my breath but he made it.

"I'll go next," Zack said confidently.

I wanted to stop him, but I didn't even try. I would be called names again.

I didn't want to watch as Zack headed out across the road as soon as there was a break in the traffic. I shut my eyes and then opened them quickly as I heard another car approaching. It seemed to me that it was going to reach us before Zack would be safely on the other side, but he fluttered out of its way just in time.

"Me next," said Clinton who could hardly wait for it to be his turn.

With a flap and a quack he was off. I could see a car coming and wanted to call out to him but it was too late. He was already out in the middle of the road. With a screech of tires, the car swerved and managed to miss Clinton as he scrambled to safety on the other side of the road.

"Your turn, Quack," they called to me.

I stood with my heart in my throat. How would I ever be able to cross and beat the fast moving cars? I waited for a good opening. Each time that I felt just about ready to go, another car would loom on the horizon and I would wait again. The fellows on the opposite side of the road began to be impatient with me.

"C'mon Quack," they called. "You had lots of time there."

"C'mon Quack, run for it. We can't wait all day."

"What you waiting for, Quack? C'mon."

At last Zack volunteered to give me a hand.

"I'll tell you when it's clear and you just run for it. Get ready. As soon as I say 'go', you go."

It sounded awfully risky to me but I prepared myself. Car after car swished by and then Zack hollered, "Go", and shutting my eyes against the danger I started across the road as fast as my legs and pumping wings could take me.

I could hear a car approaching but I still didn't open my eyes. I did not want to see it hit me. And then I was tumbling, head over tail, at the side of the road. Somehow I had made it.

I laid there for a few minutes catching my breath. The other three had already started off toward the pond. I scrambled to my feet and followed them, my heart still racing within me.

When we reached the pond the waves were high. It looked like so much fun that I almost forgot abut the busy highway. We were lifted way up in the air and then dropped again with a swoosh. Up and down, up and down. It was wonderful fun, and I didn't blame the fellows for risking their necks to come here—until I thought of the road. Then my heart would start to pound again and my body tremble. Somehow when this day's fun was over, I had to get across that road again. I dreaded the thought. I could imagine what would happen to one small duck if he were ever hit by one of those fast-moving, big cars. There would be nothing left of him. No wonder Mother and Father had warned us so many times to stay away from the highway.

But for the moment I tried to put aside all of my fears and just enjoy this wonderful time on the waves. They certainly were a lot bigger than the waves on our little pond. I could just imagine tiny Fluff being flipped high on one of these. *Why, she would look like a speck on top of it.* And then I had another thought. *Which one of us is supposed to be on guard duty for the hawk?*

Chapter Eleven

The Decision

The wind died down all too soon and our big waves soon became little waves and then hardly waves at all. We all knew that we might as well be swimming on the little pond for all of the thrill that was left. It was hard to go back to just swimming around after all of the fun that we had been having.

And then there was a swoosh and a dark figure plummeted from the sky and struck the water just as Zack ducked his head under. Now, Zack hadn't seen the hawk nor been prepared to dive to evade him. It happened that he was just going to dive to show Clinton how long he could stay under water.

As the hawk struck the spot where Zack disappeared, all three of the rest of us quickly disappeared as well. We had not been thinking nor watching for the hawk, and it was only luck, not good management, that had saved our skins.

We stayed under water for as long as we could and then nervously surfaced. The hawk swung down again and we were forced back under.

When we came up again I looked around for reeds or water plants so that we might take cover. I couldn't spot any nearby. The only plants that seemed to grow in the large pond were way across the water on the far side. It would take far too long to reach them.

We dove again and held our breath for as long as we could. I felt that my lungs would break with the effort. Again we surfaced, but only for long enough to gasp for air and then we were forced under again.

I didn't know how long we could keep this up. Surely the hawk must know that he was wearing us out. Would it just stay right there in the sky waiting for us to give up in exhaustion?

We re-surfaced for a quick breath of air and I noticed this time that the sun was sinking in the west. If anything saved us, it would be the sunset. The hawk would maybe leave us then. Yet, some birds hunted even better at night than in the daylight I had been told. I hoped with all of my heart that this hawk was not one of them.

We dove again and stayed down for as long as possible. We were too out of breath to even speak to one another as we rose to the surface again. Even the tough Clinton and Godfrey were showing signs of wear. I think that they were every bit as nervous as I was.

We kept it up. I thought that I could not possibly go on any longer with each dive that I made. I hoped that the hawk might be tiring too. It was getting quite dark now. We resurfaced warily and could just detect the hawk in the evening sky, moving off toward the west. He had given up. We had won.

The boys began to laugh and boast then about how we had outsmarted the hawk and how we were able to take care of ourselves. They bragged on and on, now that the threat had passed.

I began to think now of the wide, scary highway. It still needed to be crossed to get home. I was starving, too. We had had very little to eat. First we had been too busy having fun and then we had been too busy just staying alive. I wished with all of my heart that I had stayed home where I belonged. The thrill of the big waves was not enough to foolishly risk one's life

for.

"We'd better go," I said.

"Yeah, the waves aren't any fun anymore," agreed Clinton.

We swam to shore and picked our way back to the highway. It seemed even busier than before. The cars, with bright eyes gleaming, whooshed by with a loud roaring sound. Before one had fully passed, another was bearing down quickly upon us. I couldn't see how we'd ever make it.

"I'll go first," said Zack.

He waited for what appeared to be a break and went dashing across. He stumbled in the ditch on the other side just as a big truck whipped the weeds on the side of the road, making them wave in the wake of the wind.

"I'll go next," said Clinton, but I thought that he sounded nervous in spite of his attempt to sound tough.

He started across and then realized that he had not picked his time right. He scrambled back to safety just in time and had to wait and try again. This time, he made it. But he, too, had no room to spare.

Soon it was my turn. I could put it off no longer.

"I'll tell you when, Quack," Zack yelled back to me.

I didn't argue. I just braced myself at the side of the road, ready to make a dash for it.

As soon as Zack called, "Go," I propelled myself forward as quickly as I could, flapping and paddling my way across with all of the energy and strength that my wings and feet could produce.

I was about half way across when Zack called out in terror. "Stop, Quack! Go back! Go back!" I stopped. There was a fast-moving car bearing down upon me from the east. I turned to scurry back, but there were two cars moving in quickly from the west. I could not go back. I gave one desperate plunge forward and hoped that I would make it. I didn't. The car swished right over me, flipping me end over end. Fortunately the spinning tires did not strike me, but I was tumbled and banged until I was almost senseless.

As soon as the car sped on, I picked myself up, and reeling dizzily I hurried to the side of the road.

The fellows were waiting for me, their faces pale, their breath held, but as soon as I managed to tumble into the grass beside them, a little cheer went up.

"You made it," said Clinton.

"We knew you could," said Godfrey. "You see? It's all in the knowing how to take care of yourself."

Zack reached over and helped me to my feet. "You okay, Quack?" he asked shakily.

"Sure, he's okay," answered the all-knowing Clinton on my behalf. "He knows how to look after himself. Did you see him? He knew just how to time it."

"Won't need to be mama's boy anymore," said Godfrey.

"I think that the next time we go we should come back before dark," said Zack. "It's easier to judge the timing when you aren't blinded by the bright lights."

I picked myself up then, my head still spinning, but I was thinking clearly enough to answer Zack.

"What do you mean, the *next time* we go? There won't be a next time for me."

"Oh, c'mon Quack," said Clinton. "You gonna let one bad little experience keep you from all the fun?"

"One bad little experience?" I choked. "I nearly got killed out there. You saw it. That car nearly hit me. And that hawk. We weren't even ready for him. He almost got Zack."

"Well, he didn't," insisted Clinton.

"Well, it was too close for me," I continued. "If you guys want to risk your necks for a few rides on the waves, that's your business, but not me. Call me a sissy if you want, but at least I will be a live sissy. It's not worth the risk, that's all. And I don't care how much you tease me or coax me. I'm not going again. A fellow has the right to make up his own mind on something like this, and I've made up mine."

And so saying I started off for home and the safety of the barnyard and the food that I knew would be waiting there. Maybe the dangers of the outside world did hold excitement. I supposed that there would always be those who would just have to try them out. Well, I wouldn't be one of them. I enjoyed fun as much as anyone, but it was silly to risk so much just to get a thrill or two, and I didn't care how much the fellows poked fun at me, I wouldn't be going with them again. Mother and Father had known all along exactly what they were talking about.

Chapter Twelve

Missing

A few days passed without any excitement. I thought that things might have settled down and that the other boys had decided too that the dangerous trip across the busy highway was too risky to be taken just for the fun of a few hours of riding the waves. One windy day came and went and nothing was said about making the trip. I began to feel a little better. The next time that the wind promised to blow, Zack was at my side.

"Have you changed your mind?" he asked. "Do you want to come with us?"

"Are you going again?" I asked, finding it hard to believe.

"Of course."

"You're crazy," I told him.

"Look, Quack," he said, and I wondered as he said it just how often in the past few days he had heard the words from the other fellows. "You had a bit of bad luck. That has never happened before, and will never happen again. Besides, you made it, didn't you? I don't know why you are so uptight about it."

"Look," I told Zack, "I have no intention of going again. I've already told Father and Mother that I was sorry and wouldn't disobey again. It's risky—just like they tried to tell us, and you know it. I wish that you wouldn't go either. Something could happen, Zack. It's dangerous. Both from the cars, and the hawk."

"Nothing will happen," said Zack confidently. "We can take care of ourselves."

"I hope you're right."

"But you won't come?"

"No, I won't come."

Zack left me then and went to join Clinton and Godfrey. I saw them look my way and sneer.

"Leave the kid alone," I heard Zack say. "If he doesn't want to come, that's his business."

I appreciated Zack sticking up for me, but I did so wish that he wouldn't keep on taking chances.

I went to the pond with Mother and Father. They did not always take a count now to check if we were all with them. They knew that we were getting older and hopefully, wiser, and should take some of the responsibility for our own safety now. Yet, if we were around, they still watched out for us, ready to warn us if danger threatened.

It seemed like a long day. I watched for Zack and his friends to return. They did not come to the pond.

I was anxious to get back to the farmyard. I thought that they might be there. When we went in to feed on the scattered grain, they were not there either. I began to worry. Were they still needing to wait out the hawk? I wondered what was keeping them.

We all bedded together that night. The night was warm so we did not go inside the barn. Instead we gathered together in the protection of a small building that housed our feed. The geese family rested nearby and the other ducks came to join us.

I tried to sleep but I kept looking around for Zack. He still did not come. I finally gave up and tucked my head under my wing. It would soon be morning and I needed some rest.

When morning came I again looked for Zack. He was nowhere to be seen. Father came to me. "Your mother and I are worried," he said. "We haven't seen your brother Zackery since yesterday. Do you know where he might be?"

I could hold my tongue no longer.

"Yesterday he said that he was going with Clinton and Godfrey to the big pond across the road again," I told him. "I haven't seen any of them since."

"I see," said Father. "I met Clinton's father just a few minutes ago. He was looking for Clinton. If none of them are back yet, then perhaps we needn't worry. They might still be together and just have forgotten the time."

I wanted to believe that, but I couldn't, though hearing that Clinton wasn't back yet either made me feel a little better, for I knew that they crossed the road one at a time. Surely that was reason to hope.

Another day dragged by. Zack still did not come. I could see the worried looks in Father's and Mother's faces as they kept checking about the farm and pond. Without saying anything to worry the rest of us, they were watching for Zack.

We went in to eat of the grain at the end of the day and I still hadn't seen any of the three. It seemed very strange indeed. Surely the hawk couldn't have gotten all three of them. At least one of them should have escaped.

It wasn't until almost bedtime that I spotted Godfrey and Clinton. I looked around for Zack. He was nowhere to be seen. I hurried over to them. They saw me coming and started to move away but I rushed after them.

"When did you get back?" I asked Clinton.

"Just a few minutes ago," he answered, but he wouldn't look at me.

"Did something go wrong?" I asked him.

"Like what?" he said evasively.

"I don't know, but you were gone so long."

"Just didn't feel like coming back," he said, off-handedly. Godfrey ignored me and started to move away again.

"Where's Zack?" I asked then.

"How should I know?" said Clinton.

"He was with you."

"Was he?"

I was getting a little annoyed and a lot nervous.

"You know he was," I said. "He left with you yesterday."

"That was yesterday," said Clinton.

"But you said that you didn't come home until just now."

"I said *I* didn't. I didn't say anything about Zack."

"Are you saying that Zack came home alone?" I insisted.

Clinton shrugged his shoulders. "How do I know what Zack did? I'm not his keeper."

"You don't know where Zack is?" I asked again, not believing him.

Godfrey cut in then.

"Lay off, mama's boy," he said. "He told you he doesn't know where Zack is, didn't you hear him?"

I had heard him all right but I didn't believe him. Now that Godfrey spoke up, I doubted it still more.

"You do know," I said hotly. "I know you do. Something happened to Zack, didn't it?"

"If you're so smart," said Godfrey, "you figure it out. C'mon Clinton. Let's get out of here."

I walked away, the tears stinging my eyes. Something *had* happened to Zack, I just knew it. I should have never let him go. These guys weren't his friends. They didn't even care about him. All they thought about was their own skins. They wouldn't even share with the family what had happened to Zack.

I stumbled along to the highway and looked across the wide expanse. The cars thundered by at regular intervals. I could see nothing that gave me any clues. Perhaps I was relieved at that, but it didn't solve the mystery or make my heart ache any less.

I went back to the pond. There was nothing that I could do but watch and wait. But even as I thought that, I knew within myself that Zack wouldn't be coming back.

I wasn't the only one who kept watching. As the day went on, I could see Father and Mother many times, looking about the pond or around the farmyard. They too were watching for Zack. But Zack did not come. As the days passed and he still did not come, the watching became a sad resignation. We all knew that Zack would not be coming back. His love for adventure, even in the face of great danger, had been too risky. Zack had given his life for a few hours of riding the waves.

Chapter Thirteen

Winter

The summer days turned to fall. The leaves changed color and danced in the arms of the wind. Many of them fell, twisting and turning, into the small pool. The days were shorter and the nights cooler now. We fed more and more on the grain in the yard and less and less on the small insects and grubs in the pool. We still spent much of our day swimming, but the food was just not as plentiful.

We were nearly full grown now. Oscar was almost as big as Father. He took great pride in the fact. Fluff was still small for her age, but she too had grown.

We were not supervised nearly as closely now. Prudence was the only one that stayed close to Mother, and Gertrude was not only bossing the other family members, but the other fowl of the farmyard as well.

Hiram was still the late one at whatever was done. He wandered slowly to the pool after the rest of us had been there for several minutes. Then when we left and went back to the yard to feed, he came wandering in when most of us had finished. It didn't seem to perturb him that the best picking was already taken. Hazel still preferred to take the easy way out and always choose to eat where the grain was the most plentiful and choose to swim when the waves were the least troublesome. Some days she just sat on the shore in the sun with her head tucked under her wing while the rest of us took our exercise. I was beginning to wonder if Hazel was really lazy or just plain smart. Boyd was just Boyd. Neither big nor small, neither energetic nor lazy, neither fun nor friction. He seemed to fit in well with any group without being the leader or without being a noticeable follower. He was just there.

I still missed Zack. Clinton and Godfrey came and went. I assumed that they were still going back and forth to the big pond. And then one day Godfrey was all alone. I wanted to ask him about it, but I just couldn't bring myself to do so. I watched and waited, hoping that Clinton would turn up, but he did not ever join us again either in the farmyard nor on the smaller pond.

The fall days passed by. Our pond got colder and colder. On a few mornings the surface was partly covered by a firm glaze. I asked father about it.

"It's ice," he said. "That means that winter will soon be here. In the winter months the pond freezes over entirely."

"How do we swim?"

"We don't. In the winter we have to content ourselves with being inside."

"Inside? Like the chickens?"

"We share their chicken house."

I hated the thought of that. I had always been used to my daily swim on the pond. I had always felt sorry for the chickens, locked in their pens as they were, and now Father was saying that in the winter we, too, would be shut in. I didn't care at all for the idea.

"Isn't there some way to melt the ice so that we can still swim?" I asked hoping that someone might find a way.

Father shook his head. "No," he said. "It gets too cold for too long. We couldn't possibly keep it open."

I decided to swim as much as possible while the water was still there. Some mornings it was really cold and I would have to walk out on the ice for several feet before I found open water. The ice was very slippery and more than once I took embarrassing falls. I did hope that no one was looking. It was not very dignified to be scooting across the ice on one's underside.

Then one day when we got up and came out of the big barn the whole world looked different. It was covered with a fine, duck-downy blanket of white. I had never seen anything like it before and asked Gertrude, who was standing near me, if she knew what it was.

"Of course silly," she said. "It's foam."

"So much? Where did it come from?"

"Foam comes from the waves when the wind blows hard," she said, "so I guess the wind must have blown very hard last night."

"I don't think that it could blow *that* much," I said doubtfully, thinking back to the big open pond and the high waves. There had only been very small amounts of foam along the shore.

Gertrude tossed her head. "Well, if you don't believe me, don't ask me," she said indignantly, and waddled off.

I went to Mother. "What is all this stuff?" I asked her.

"It's snow."

"Snow? Where'd it come from?"

"From the sky."

I looked up at the sky. There was no snow coming now.

"Like rain?" I asked again.

"Yes, like rain. Only snow doesn't run away and make puddles. This stays where it falls, unless the wind blows it."

Now that I had the answer I was anxious to explore the snow. I hurried out into it. It was cold, very cold. I hadn't gone far when my feet began to protest against it's coldness. Still, I determined to have another swim while the pond remained open, so I continued down the trail that I always took.

The snow was deep and hard to walk through. I think that I preferred the rain. Whose idea was this snow anyway? What was it good for and why did people want it?

When I got to the pond the ice was heavy all along the shore. I knew that I would need to walk out upon it to find open water. I started out. The snow was on the pond, too. Right on top of the ice. I walked and walked until I had crossed the pond and came to the other side. I still had not found open water. I walked back across, thinking that maybe I missed it. There *was* no open water. The whole pond was covered with ice and snow. With deep disappointment I headed back to the farmyard. There would be no more swimming. We would be locked up like the chickens. No more pond. No more tasty treats from the waters. No more fun playing in the waves or diving beneath the surface.

When I got back to the farmyard, I met Oscar.

"There's no more water," I informed him. "It's all ice and snow."

"I could have told you that," said Oscar. "All of the swimming fowl have been talking about nothing else all morning. Winter is here."

"Winter?"

"Yeah, winter."

"Does anyone like winter?" I asked.

"I don't know."

"Haven't you heard them say? What do they say about it?"

"Well, they say that it's cold, and we all get locked in. We have to eat just grain. No green things for geese. No grasshoppers for turkeys. No swimming for us."

"It doesn't sound to me like they like it," I said.

Oscar thought for a moment. "I never heard anyone say that they liked it. It sounds like they wish it wasn't coming."

"Then why do they order it?"

"I don't think that they do. I think that it just comes."

"Well why doesn't someone stop it?"

Oscar shrugged his shoulders. "Maybe the farmer likes it," he answered.

When I saw the farmer later chopping ice from the cows watering trough, and carrying large loads of split wood, and hauling much more feed to the pigs than he normally carried, I wondered why he liked the winter.

Later in the day I saw the farmer's boy. He had a funny sliding thing and he would carry it up a nearby hill and then go swishing down, yelling all the way from the top to the bottom, the big farm dog fast on his heels, barking and yelping. *Maybe they had ordered the snow,* I thought. *They certainly do seem to be having lots of fun in it.*

The next day it was even colder. I thought that maybe it

wouldn't be so bad to be shut up in the warm building with the chickens after all. It certainly was cold out, and I was cold, too. Not just my feet, which I couldn't get out of the snow, but my whole body.

The following days were colder still. I wished with all of my heart that the farmer would decide that it was time for us to be shut in out of the wind and snow.

I guess that he decided that it was time, for he came with a pail of food and coaxed us toward the big henhouse. We followed willingly. I think that we would have followed even without him tempting us with the food.

Even before we got through the door I could feel the welcome warmth and hurried forward. I wondered if the chickens resented the intrusion. They didn't seem to mind. They had their roosts and could stay above the noise and commotion that we, the ducks and geese, made. The turkeys joined the chickens on the roost. They were big birds so it was good that there was plenty of room for them.

There were pans of warm water and lots of troughs of grain. It was much easier to feed without having to peck and scratch in the snow. And it was much nicer having water that didn't turn to ice a few minutes after it had been poured in the dish. I didn't care much for winter. I had much preferred the summer or the fall. I talked to Mother about it.

"I liked the summer much better," I told her.

"I like summer, too," she said.

"Why did we have to change?" I asked.

"That's the way it is," she informed me. "Spring, summer, fall, winter. They come in that order every year."

"You mean that summer will come again? It won't always be winter now?"

"Oh, my," said Mother. "Where did you get that idea?" Then she hurried on, "Well, of course you wouldn't know. You have never seen winter before. You were hatched in the spring, and lived through your first summer and fall. Now you are into winter. It will be with us for a few months and then we will be back to spring again."

I had never heard such good news. Winter would not always be with us. Spring would be back, and closely following spring would be summer. I settled in. *I'll be able to endure this for awhile. At least we are all warm and comfortable.* I looked at the dishes filled to the brim with grain. *And well fed,* I decided.

Chapter Fourteen

Neighbors

Now that we were all sharing the same building, I got much better acquainted with the farmyard fowl. When we had been out about the yard it was easy to avoid them and stay with my own family. Now that we shared the same building, we found that in order to live in unity we had to get to know our neighbors.

This seemed to be no problem for Mother. She seemed to enjoy her times of sitting in the sun that streamed in the window and chatting with the other mothers. At first their talk was mostly about their children. They all liked to brag a bit about how we had all grown and the abilities that we showed in our swimming, diving, gobbling or crowing. Mother was no different. She bragged right along with the rest of them.

Daily, the farmer's boy came to the henhouse to gather the eggs, and daily, someone came to bring our food and water. Somedays it was the farmer, sometimes his wife, but most often it was the boy. Once in a while the farm dog came in with him, and then there was a great commotion in the coop as hens squawked and scrambled, and turkeys flapped their way to the highest rung of the roost. We ducks and geese could only run to get out of his way, calling out to warn one another as we did so. I don't think that the boy was supposed to bring the dog in the coop with him, for when the noise began to get loud, he hurried to get the dog out again.

One of the geese was a large, white, mothery-person. She was called, affectionately, Granny, by all of the fowl. Even the turkeys called her that, and that was something, for the turkeys were inclined to be a bit offish. They seemed to feel that because of their bigness and their bright coloring, they were just a little bit better than the rest of us.

But Granny was a favorite with all of us. She never fussed or scolded, but was interested in each one of us. She was the storyteller of the household, too. Each night, just as the sun was dipping down behind the distant hills, the young goslings would gather around Granny coaxing for a story, and those of us who wished to could sneak in close and listen as well. And it wasn't just the geese and ducks either. Nor was it just the young. I often saw the older birds with their heads cocked as they listened to the story. The ducks, geese, chickens, and even the turkeys, though they often pretended no interest, sat with heads tipped slightly to the side so that they wouldn't miss a word.

The winter nights were long, the days short, and so Granny's stories were welcomed. Most often they were about her experiences as she remembered them. Granny was the oldest fowl on the farm and she had much to tell of how things used to be. Even the sparrows in the rafters, who came and went all day long, made sure that they were there for story hour.

I never did get to know all of the chickens. There were too many of them, and besides, they all looked alike to me. The hens were always busy, scratching and clucking their way about the coop. Much of their day was spent sitting on their nests producing the eggs that the boy always came looking for. The younger chickens squabbled and played in turn. They seemed to always be looking for something to do. They were of a variety of colors and you could never tell by their looks which family they belonged to.

There seemed to be a great rivalry among the roosters. When one crowed, another threw back his head and crowed even louder, then another would stand on the perch and try to outdo him. The biggest rooster seemed to think that he was the boss of the place. He strutted about, making sure that everyone else knew his proper place. I thought him a rather arrogant fellow, but Mother said that every place needs a controller to keep things in order. She said that the henhouse, too, needed someone in charge. I certainly wasn't going to challenge the big fellow, but one or two of the cockier younger roosters sometimes did. When they did, a fight would result. They would face one another, their neck feathers raised and shout insults, and strike at one another as they leaped in the air, kicking up feathers and dust from the bottom of the coop. Sometimes it went on and on until I felt that one or the other must surely drop from exhaustion. I was glad that I wasn't called upon to enter the fray. I was also glad when they finally decided to stop.

When a fight was taking place, most of the other fowl went about their way as though nothing of import was happening, and maybe nothing of import was. Even the hens ignored it and clucked their way across the coop, picking up scattered grain as they went. When the fight was finally over, no one congratulated the winner nor consoled the loser. Life just went on.

The turkeys didn't talk to us much. They talked to one another a lot though, in loud gobbley voices. They spent most of their time feeding. They had mammoth appetites and it seemed to take most of their time just filling their hungry stomachs. Even the young ones seemed to stay to themselves. If they talked to anyone, it was with some of the younger chickens.

Our family members stayed mostly with the other ducks, though we often chatted with the geese. We got to know the other young ducks quite well. In fact, they seemed like very fine folk. Clinton's brother, Horace, and I often chatted. When we got to know one another, we shared our thoughts and concerns about our missing brothers. I confessed to Horace that I had gone with the boys to the pond one day and how scary it had been to cross the busy highway. Horace said that they had coaxed him on more than one occasion and that he had been tempted to try it, but had known that his folks would disapprove. Neither of us cared much for Godfrey and avoided him whenever we could. We were both sure that he knew exactly what had happened to our brothers but was not talking. We got to be real good friends, Horace and I.

Horace had some sisters, too. They were Agnes, and Hilda, and Petunia, and Constance, but as the winter went on it was Abigail who caught my eye.

She was a pretty little thing, and shy. She spent a lot of time with Fluff. The two seemed to be really good friends. I noticed some of the other young ducks watching Abigail as well. I knew that she was a favorite and felt that I had very little chance of getting her attention. I wished that winter would hurry and be over so that I might be turned out and not kept so closely confined. I didn't see how I could possibly get Abigail to notice me with so many others around.

I often saw Oscar showing off for her benefit. She didn't pay too much attention to him and for that I was thankful.

The winter days dragged on. There was not much to do for excitement. There was no swimming, no diving, no hunting for bugs. One could not even take much of a walk.

All that we did was eat, sleep and talk. The biggest event of the day was Granny's story hour. I began to get very bored with life. I decided that I would like a chance to get out, even if it meant cold feet, but there was never a chance. The farmer, or his wife or son, were always careful to close the door firmly behind them after they had cared for us.

"Stop fretting, Quackery," said Mother one day, after watching me fidgeting. "It won't be long until spring will be here."

I did so hope that she was right. I was so tired of winter. I think that all of the fowl were tired of being cooped up. Fights often broke out, even amcng the more docile birds.

The sparrows brought the first words of hope.

"The brook is starting to run," they said excitedly. "Just a trickle, but it's a good sign."

I went to the window to look out but my neck wasn't long enough.

More days went by.

"The crows are back," said the biggest rooster. "I heard them cawing this morning just after I crowed to wake up the farm."

We still waited.

"The snow is melting," said Mrs. Red, the oldest hen in the coop. "There's a little wet patch in the corner where it runs in each spring."

Still we waited.

"The ground is almost bare," said the turkey, craning his neck to look out of the window from his perch on the roost.

A cheer went up.

"When will they let us out?" I asked Mother, impatiently.

"When they know that it's time," she assured me. "Any day now."

It seemed like such a long time since I had a good swim. I wondered if I would still know how. My whole body ached to be out of this coop and into the fresh air. The others must have shared my feelings. We had been locked up for long enough.

Chapter Fifteen

Spring

One morning the farmer came to the door and held it open wide. "C'mon," he called. "Out you go."

We did not wait for a second invitation. As one, we all moved for the door, hurrying out before he had a chance to change his mind. Even the chickens were allowed out into the sunshine. They flapped their way excitedly over our heads. The turkeys, too, went out with flapping wings and chuckles of delight. The geese hurried next. They were bigger than we were and could push their way around. We, the ducks, were the last to scurry through the door. We hurried out as quickly as we could, pushing one another in our eagerness to be out in the open.

It was a very different world that welcomed us. The snow still lay around in banks near the buildings and fences. The rest of the yard was muddy and wet. There were no leaves on the trees and no grass on the ground. All looked brown and bare, but it still looked good to me. I was tired of looking at four wooden walls.

At once I hurried to the pond, anxious for that long-awaited swim. It was still frozen when I reached the shore so I waded out upon the ice, wondering how far I would need to go until I found open water. There was none. I was so disappointed. I had wanted a swim for so long and I still would not be able to have one.

I went back to the farmyard, dejectedly. I found Horace in a puddle. It was hardly deep enough to lift his body and yet he swam round and round in the middle of the little bit of water, enjoying himself immensely. He saw me looking at him with envy in my eyes. "Come on in," he called. "It's not very big but it's better than nothing."

I hurried to join him. As the sun climbed into the sky our puddle grew. By the afternoon, Fluff and Abigail had joined us in our own private little swimming pool. We had wonderful fun, though there was no way that we could practice our diving skills. In fact we had to swim, round and round, nose to tail in order to even fit.

We were sure that on the next day our puddle would be even bigger. There were still snowdrifts nearby that needed to melt, and with the warm spring sun working on them, we would have a good-sized puddle in no time.

The next morning we hurried to the puddle to be sure that no one else had found it and beat us to it. We were disappointed. There was no water at all. Where we had had a puddle the day before, all that we had was a patch of ice. We turned away in sadness and went back to the farmyard for food. I didn't even feel hungry.

Abigail passed closely by me and, noticing my dejection, spoke in an effort to cheer me up.

"It'll be here again as soon as the sun comes up."

I cheered some, more from the fact that she spoke to me than from the message she brought.

"Do you really think so?" I asked her.

"Sure. It's early yet. It always freezes again over night."

I knew that she was right. It was early. Yet it wasn't so early that the sun shouldn't already be up. The sky was still a mass of clouds, with no sun shining. I was afraid that something was awfully wrong, that things might be all mixed up. It was supposed to be spring, but today did not look like spring at all.

A few hours later I was even more sure, for it started to snow again. Now I was really alarmed. I looked for Father or Mother. Something should be done. We were headed for another winter and we had only spring for one day, and no summer or fall at all.

I found Mother visiting with Granny Goose. I waited for a moment so that I would not interrupt.

"You wanted to talk to me, Quackery?" asked Mother.

"For just a minute," I told her, wanting to assure her that she could resume her visit as soon as I had asked my question.

"What is it?" she asked.

"Look," I said, "it's snowing."

"I had noticed," she said, unconcerned.

"But it's supposed to be spring," I insisted.

"Yes," said Mother. "It's spring."

"But it's snowing," I said again. "It's supposed to snow in winter, not in spring."

"Oh, it snows in spring, too, Quackery. Often."

"It does?"

"Sure it does. It just doesn't get as cold or last as long."

"But I thought—" I stopped.

"Don't worry son. It won't last long. The snow will fall for a while and then the sun will come out again and melt it away. It comes and goes in the springtime, but spring will finally make it. It'll come. And close on its heels will be summer."

Mother seemed so sure of herself that my mind was put at ease. But I still didn't like it. I wanted no more snow, not for a very long time. Yet if it happened over and over each spring, then I might as well accept it. I decided to go look for Horace and the other young ducks. Maybe we could think of something to do while we waited for spring to come back again.

Mother was right. It soon stopped snowing, though the sun still did not shine. It did return on the next day, though, and our puddle began to grow again. It wasn't until the next day that it was big enough to hold ducks and then we had to take turns.

The following day it could hold five of us at a time, though it was still very crowded, and finally we could all get in together though we scarcely had room to move and it was still much too shallow for diving. Still, it was a way to help fill our days until the pond would be open for swimming. Daily we sent out scouts to check on the pond's progress. It seemed like the news was always the same, but then one day, Oscar, whose turn it had been to check things out, came rushing back all out of breath.

"It's open!" he cried as he ran flapping toward us. "It's open!"

And sure enough, it was. Oh, not a very big patch of water

but enough so that we could get our bodies in and splash about. We could even dive, though we had to watch that we didn't come up under the ice.

As we swam back and forth enjoying every minute of it, the circle of water became bigger and bigger. Darkness came far too soon that night. I was tempted to stay right there where I was, so afraid I was that the cold night air would close up our pond again. It almost did, too, but with our moving bodies and the warmth of the sun we soon had it open again. Spring was really coming. We just needed to be patient, that was all.

Chapter Sixteen

Changes

The days began to get warmer and warmer. The snowdrifts began to shrink and the puddles to expand. The pond water was increasing daily in size while the ice that covered the sides was getting less and less.

Many birds were appearing around the farmyard and in the nearby trees. They all talked excitedly about nesting time and where to stop for the best materials.

One day as I hurried off to join my friends at the pond, I met Mother. She was carrying a piece of straw in her bill and as I watched, she crossed to a hidden area and deposited it carefully on a pile of many other straws. I realized that the pile on the ground was beginning to look like our old nest had looked.

"What are you doing?" I asked her.

She looked up in surprise but she answered me, "Building a nest."

"But I—I—"

"Yes?" she asked.

"Well, it's just that I don't think that I want to live there anymore."

Mother began to laugh softly. "You?" she said. "No, my

foolish little one. You will not be living here."

I felt relief.

"Then why do you build a nest?" I asked, perplexed.

"For me," she said, "And your father."

I was really confused then. If she was building it for her and Father then why was I not to live there also?

"I don't understand," I said, "I thought that you said that I wouldn't be living there."

"And so you won't," she said, without even looking up. She was much too busy arranging each twig and straw just so.

"Then why? Why bother to build if we—"

"Father and I are building the nest for our new family. You are full grown now. You will have a nest of your own."

"But I—I—don't even know how to build a nest," I stammered.

Mother smiled.

"You'll know," she said evenly, "when the time comes."

"And I don't have anyone to live with," I went on uncertainly.

"You'll find someone."

"When?"

"When it's the proper time."

I was really puzzled. I had never really thought of the future. I guess I hadn't expected things to change, but they were changing, very quickly, it seemed.

Father soon came and in his bill he also carried straw.

"What do you want?" he said rather gruffly.

"I just wanted to talk to Mother."

"She's busy," said Father, and I got a strange feeling that I wasn't expected to stay around.

"I'm just off for a swim," I said hastily. "I'll see you around."

There was no answer from either Father or Mother. They were too busy tucking and poking around the new nest. Puzzling over what it all meant I hurried off to the pond.

We had a wonderful time swimming and diving. I noticed

again what a pretty picture Abigail made as she rode the crests of the waves.

That evening when we went to the yard to feed, Father and Mother did not ask us to join them. I wondered if the rest of the family noticed. Prudence did, for when she went to join Mother at bedtime, Father sent her back to stay with Gertrude and Hazel.

In the days that followed I did not see much of either Mother or Father. I noticed that some of the other farmyard fowl were missing as well, and whenever anyone asked of their whereabouts the answer was always the same, "They're nesting."

I did a great deal of puzzling over this strange turn of events. It seemed that all around us there were creatures who were 'nesting.'

I looked for Fluff. I needed someone to talk to.

I met her down by the pond. She seemed in a great hurry.

"Can we talk?" I asked her.

"Of course," she said, "but I only have a minute."

"You look all excited," I said to her.

"I am," she flushed. "I've been out looking for a nesting site and I've found a good one."

"A nesting site?" I echoed. "You don't find a nesting site all alone."

"Silly," she said. "Horace has asked me to share a nest with him. We've both been looking for a place to build our nest and I've found just the place."

"Really?" I couldn't believe it.

"Really."

"When will you start?"

"It's too late to start building today. We'll start first thing in the morning."

"Well," I said, knowing that I couldn't hold her any longer, "I wish you the best. Both of you. I like Horace. He's a nice fellow."

"Thank you, Quackery," said Fluff. "I wish you well, too."

"But I'm not nesting."

"You will," she said with confidence. "And I would advise you not to wait too long. Nearly all of the good sites have been taken."

And she hurried off to find Horace and tell him her good news.

Now I felt more alone than ever. Mother and Father were gone. They were far too preoccupied with their nest to pay attention to the rest of us. The family members of the other fowl were also busy building nests, and now Fluff, my little sister, was going to be busy building her nest as well.

I wandered toward the pond, my head down. Maybe a good swim would help to clear my brain.

I was almost to the pond when a voice stopped me.

"What's wrong?" It was Abigail.

I jerked to a stop and tried to smile.

"Oh, hi, Abbie. Oh, nothing really. I was just thinking."

"Well, you were certainly very deep in thought. I thought for a moment that you might run over me without even seeing me."

"I'm sorry," I apologized. "I guess I was pretty deep in thought at that."

"Do you want to go for a swim?" asked Abigail.

"Would you mind?"

"I'd love to," said Abigail, who slid into the water very gracefully and glided away.

I joined her.

"Now," she said after we had swam in silence for a few minutes, "would you like to talk about whatever it was that you were thinking so deeply about?"

I smiled at her. I didn't know where to start.

"Are your folks around?" I asked her.

"Well, yes and no," said Abigail. "They are not far off, but they are busy so I don't see much of them."

"Nesting?"

"That's right."

"Did you notice that most of the fowl in the farmyard are nesting?"

"I noticed."

I swam in silence for a few more minutes. Abbie swam silently at my side.

"My folks are nesting again, too." I said at last.

"I know," said Abigail. "Prudence told me. She feels rather lonely."

I guess I felt rather lonely too, though I wasn't ready to confess it to Abigail, or anyone for that matter.

"Do you?" I finally asked.

"Do I what?" she said, puzzled.

"Do you feel sort of lonely now that your folks are nesting again?"

"Maybe—a little."

"Guess I do too," I said, knowing that there was no use trying to hide it.

We continued circling the pond.

"Are you worried about it?" asked Abigail.

"Worried? No. I'm not worried. It just takes some getting used to, that's all."

"What will you do?"

I laughed at that. It was rather a silly question. After all, I was full grown now, I didn't need my father and my mother to care for me anymore.

"I don't know. Just hang around, I guess."

There was silence again.

"Did you hear about Fluff and Horace?" I said to change the subject, but it really didn't change the subject at all.

"You mean that they are building a nest, too?"

"Yeah," I muttered.

"Yes, I heard. Fluff was all excited when I met her a few minutes ago."

"She sure was," I agreed.

"That's what you should do too," Abigail said.

"What?"

"Build a nest."

"Me? I don't even have anyone to build a nest with. You don't just build a nest on your own, you know."

"I know," said Abigail, very coyly, and I suddenly realized that I was being prompted, ever so gently.

I cleared my throat, but it was awfully hard to know what to say and how to say it. I cleared my throat again. Abigail just waited.

"Do you think—" I began, then started over. "Would you be interested, I mean, are you planning to—to—build a nest?"

"I hope to—some day," said Abbie, and then repeated my words, with a charming smile. "You don't just build a nest on your own, you know."

"Well, do you have anyone to—to—plans that is, with anyone?"

"Not yet."

I really swallowed hard now.

"Would you care—to—to—ah—build it with me?" I hurried through the final words, prepared to make a dash for it if Abigail turned me down.

Her smile deepened. She flashed it directly at me and my heart started thumping.

"I'd love to, Quackery," she said, and then almost under her breath, "I thought you'd never ask."

Chapter Seventeen

Choosing A Site

We began our search for a building site first thing the next morning. I knew now why Fluff had been so excited. I felt the same way. There was great anticipation in the thought of having one's own nest.

We discussed whether we should go together or each look in a different direction. We knew that building sites were quickly being taken with so many of the farmyard fowl looking for places to build. Though our practical side told us that it might be wiser to go our separate ways, we decided to go together. It would be so much more fun that way.

We set out in high spirits, chatting as we went. Fluff had been right. Most of the good spots were already taken.

By mid-morning we were becoming concerned. We didn't want to be too far from the farmyard because of the feeding, and we did not want to be too far away from the buildings, because of the protection they offered from enemies who might creep in, and we certainly didn't want to be too far away from the pond, for new, little legs would not be able to walk too great a distance and our young ducklings would be taken to the water soon after they had hatched. There just didn't seem to be many sites left with all three of those things considered. We were forced to range out further and further.

The sun was high in the sky and we still hadn't found a place. We stopped hurriedly to eat and then prepared to set out again.

"Maybe Fluff is right," said Abbie, "Maybe we should split up and you should go one way and I another."

I knew that she was right, though I hated to do it that way. I agreed rather reluctantly.

"If you think that's best."

So she went off toward the far side of the pond and I scouted around the farm buildings.

When we met back at the farmyard at dusk, we were both feeling rather dejected. Neither of us had found what we felt to be a suitable place.

"What will we do?" asked Abbie, in a tired and disappointed voice.

I tried to cheer her up. "We'll look again tomorrow," I said, as though it would be easy to find something on the new day.

She still looked rather sad but she tried to smile at me.

"There must be lots of places," I continued, "we just haven't discovered them yet."

"There must be," she repeated.

After we had found our place to sleep among the rest of the flock, I still couldn't fall asleep. In my mind I went over every square inch of the territory that I had covered during the day, testing again to see if I had missed a potential nesting place.

The tree by the pig lot? No, it was on too much of a slant. The ground fell away sharply there. The tall grass by the fence? No, it was far too low. The nest would be flooded with every rain. The west bank of the pond? No, it was far too open. Every hawk in the sky would spot us there. The end of the calf pasture? No, it was all rocks. It would never make a comfortable nest.

Over and over in my mind I reviewed the places that I had

seen. None of them seemed suitable.

We'll just have to try again tomorrow, I told myself and tucked my head deeper under my wing in an effort to put it all from my mind and get some sleep.

It must have worked, for the next thing that I was conscious of was the morning sun streaming down upon us as it climbed from its bed.

Abbie was anxious to be off. I tried to slow her down. "First," I told her, "we must have some breakfast. It's going to be a busy day and we must eat if we are going to be able to do all that must be done."

She agreed, but she ate hurriedly. I was afraid that she would have indigestion.

We started out then. We decided to try searching together again. It hadn't worked for us to look separately anyway so we might as well travel together. Abbie was to watch carefully on our right side and I was to check everything on the left.

There didn't seem to be much. We walked on past the chicken coop and along the rail fence. Now and then we stopped and checked a site that looked like it might have possibilities, but there was always something wrong with it. I began to think that we might be too picky.

It was almost noon when we came to a spot in a clump of willows not too far from the waters of the pond. We looked at the site and then looked at each other. It looked ideal. We moved closer. It was perfect.

We began to beam at one another.

"It's great," I stated.

"Wonderful," said Abbie.

"Look. It's nice and close to the pond, too."

"It couldn't be better," but for some reason the smile was slowly fading from Abbie's face.

I could see her looking around, this way and that, and it made me a bit impatient with her.

"Don't you like it? I thought that you said it was wonderful."

"It is," said Abbie, and there was real concern in her eyes now.

"So?" I prompted.

"So—why hasn't someone else grabbed it?" spoke Abbie. "There's something wrong with it or it would have been taken."

"Oh, c'mon," I said a bit peevishly. "Don't look for problems where none exist."

But she went right on looking.

"I'm sure that there is something wrong," she continued. "It wouldn't be left sitting here like this if there wasn't. There are too many looking for sites and this one is just too good a one. There must be something wrong."

I didn't agree with her, but what could I say.

Abbie began to scout around to look for clues.

"There has never been a nest here," she stated, "at least not for a very long time."

"So, no one has found it before."

"It couldn't be missed, Not this close to the pond and the buildings. It's something else. I just know it."

"I think that we should be thankful and not waste anymore time." I stated, trying to do so as gently as I could.

Abbie really wasn't listening.

"It's pretty wet," she stated.

"A lot of places are a little wet yet. There hasn't been enough time for the sun to properly dry them out since the snow has melted."

"I don't know," hesitated Abbie.

"Well, make up your mind. If we don't use this one, we must keep looking."

I was beginning to wonder if we'd ever find anything that would please Abbie, but I didn't say so.

"I think—," began Abbie and then stopped to do just that. She stood there tipping her head this way and that, looking at the nest site from every angle.

"Well?" I prompted again, hoping that she would say that she'd take it.

She didn't.

"I think that we should keep on looking," she said instead. "Something about this just isn't right."

I wanted to argue with her, but I bit my tongue. We'd keep looking but I was sure that we'd never find anything better and in the meantime, someone else would move in here.

Well, it would be Abbie's doing. I would try not to say, "I told you so," but I did hope that she'd realize it herself.

We went on, trudging our way around the farm. It was a tiring, unpleasant task. I would have much rather been swimming. For some reason the excitement had gone out of nest building.

"I think that we should stop for something to eat," I said at last.

Abbie sighed and looked at the sky. The sun was high above us.

"You're right," she agreed, hesitantly. "Boy, do my feet hurt!"

We waddled back to the farmyard. Both of us were weary and discouraged. If I had known how much effort it was going to take to find the proper place to build a nest, I might have thought twice about asking Abbie to nest with me.

We didn't talk much to the other fowl. I guess all of us had our minds on other things.

We had finished eating and were taking a few minutes to rest when one of the young geese came flapping excitedly into the yard.

"I've found it. I've found it," she screeched to her male partner.

"Finally," he said with a heavy sigh and sat right down on the ground.

The young goose turned to the turkey who fed nearby and explained, all flushed and wild with excitement. "I've found the perfect spot. I mean, *perfect*. We've been looking for three days and now I've found it. I can't believe that it hasn't been taken already. Come on Greyboy, we must hurry and get back to it before someone else takes it."

The turkey hen did not seem impressed, though she did smile kindly.

"Where is it?" she asked to be sociable.

"Right over there. Right over there in the willow bushes."

I looked at Abbie, with a real I-told-you-so look in spite of my resolve, and she looked at me with a plea for forgiveness. But the turkey didn't seem to be awfully impressed. She took another gobble of grain and then said very calmly, "You can't build there, dear."

The young goose stopped mid-stride.

"And why not?" she asked rather hotly. "I found it—and it's not marked. If someone else wanted it—"

But the turkey cut in. "Oh, I'm sure that no one else wants it."

The goose looked puzzled.

"Is it wet?" asked the turkey.

"Well, yes. Right now it is. But it will soon dry out. The sun hasn't even gotten to it yet. In a day or so—"

"No," said the turkey hen," it won't dry out. You see, there is a little underground spring there and it just keeps on seeping and seeping all year round. It never dries out any more than it is right now."

I felt sorry for the young goose. Her face fell and she looked about to cry. The young gander didn't look much better. He knew that the search would need to continue.

I took my eyes off them and looked back at Abbie. There was a hint of triumph showing in her eyes, but she didn't even say anything.

We got up slowly and went searching again.

Chapter Eighteen

Nest Building

We ended another day with nothing. Though we had searched and searched, we still hadn't found what we were looking for. I was beginning to give up but Abbie kept pushing on. After what had happened at the willows, I no longer argued with her when she rejected a site. I felt that she probably knew more what she was looking for than I did.

We trudged on and on, and came up empty.

That night when we went to bed I did not even bother to review the sites that we had looked at that day. For one thing, there was getting to be far too many of them for me to remember, and for another, if Abbie had already turned them down, there wasn't any use looking at them again anyway. I tucked my head under my wing and went right to sleep. I would need all of the rest that I could get to face another day of house-shopping.

Abbie didn't spend long eating the next morning either. She did say that if I was too weary, she'd go looking on her own. I was tempted to accept her offer, but I knew that the nest was my responsibility too, and so, grumpily I'm afraid, I went along.

We spent the morning around the farmyard. There just didn't seem to be anything near the pond. It seemed that all the ducks and geese liked a lakeside view and we had been too late in getting started.

Just when I was about to give up, Abbie spotted a place. My hopes began to raise as she studied it carefully.

"A little far from the pond," she stated, "but maybe not too far. We could walk slowly. Doesn't have as much cover as I would like, but maybe it's not too open. It is nice and high and would stay dry, and it's nice and smooth for building. Rain shouldn't be a problem and wind shouldn't bother it too much. It's close enough to the buildings that predators shouldn't have easy access. It might do."

I could have shouted, but I stayed calm, hoping with all of my heart that Abbie would not change her mind.

She looked around carefully. "Yes," she said finally, "It'll be just fine."

I breathed a deep sigh of relief.

"What should we do first?" I asked then, letting Abbie take the lead.

"You may go eat," she said. "I'll stay here. I don't want to lose it. When you are finished, I'll go eat."

That seemed like a smart plan to me. I didn't want to lose it, either.

"Why don't you go first?" I said to Abbie. "I'll wait."

Abbie smiled a thank you and went off to the farmyard. It didn't take her long and she was back again.

"Your turn," she said sweetly.

"How could you eat so quickly?" I asked. "Are you sure that you had enough?"

"I wasn't very hungry," said Abbie.

I didn't know if she was just excited or wanted to get back quickly for my sake. Maybe it was some of both.

"I'll see you in a few minutes," I said and started off.

I had not gone far when Abbie called after me, "Quack?"

I turned.

"Do you like it?" she asked, concern in her voice.

"I think it's great," I assured her, fearing that she might start searching all over again.

"Good," she smiled, relieved. "I was hoping you'd like it."

I returned her smile and then took another two steps.

"Quack?"

Again I turned, wondering if I'd ever get my dinner.

"Would you mind bringing back some straw when you come? We might as well get started."

I smiled again. "Sure," I said. "I'll bring some straw,"

When I returned from eating my dinner, carrying the straw that Abbie had asked for, she had already been busy gathering bits of grass and nearby material for the nest. It didn't look like much of a pile yet and I knew that she must have been working hard all of the time I was gone. It made me realize what a big job building the nest was going to be.

I laid down my straw and turned to go for more.

"I'll work around here," said Abbie, "so I can keep an eye on the nest. You can bring straw from the farmyard. It's much more plentiful there."

And so we began our serious task of preparing our first nest. I had no idea just how it was done, but Abbie seemed to know instinctively. I carried the material to her and she added it to what she had found around the nest site and had very carefully tucked it into place.

When evening came we had a good start, but were far from finished. I looked to Abbie for direction.

"We'd better stop and feed and get some rest," she said. "We'll continue in the morning."

I agreed, only too happy to take a break.

We walked to the farmyard. I looked at Abbie. She had a delightful smug look about her and I knew that she was happy. It made me feel happy, too. I was proud of her, too. She was doing such a good job of setting everything up just right. I wasn't sorry now that I had asked her to nest with me. It was worth every bit of the trouble.

We reached the farmyard and took our time eating. Abbie seemed much more content now. I supposed that it was the first time all day that she really had had time to enjoy her meal.

After eating our fill, we snuggled down together in the shelter of the big barn with the rest of the fowl. It had been a good day. We were getting settled. We would soon have a nest of our own.

The next morning we were up early and soon to work. I had had no idea how many straws and bits of grass and fallen feathers it took to build a nest. All day long we worked together and still when nightfall came we weren't finished.

"It's taking shape," said Abbie.

I knew that she was tired. Yet she still seemed very pleased with the world. I was glad that she wasn't fussing.

Fluff and Horace sat close beside us when we went to rest for the night.

"Did you find a place yet?" asked Fluff.

Abbie beamed. "Yesterday."

"Good," said Fluff. "I'm so happy for you. It's such a chore finding the right spot."

I agreed wholeheartedly but said nothing. Horace and I just exchanged looks.

"Have you finished building?" asked Abbie now.

"Almost," said Fluff, excitedly.

Abbie sighed. "We still have a long ways to go," she said, "but it's coming."

"It comes along quickly after you get the foundation laid," Horace assured us.

I was glad to hear that.

Still, it took us three more days of very hard work until the nest suited Abbie.

Chapter Nineteen

Disappointments

The next task for Abbie was to fill the newly built nest with the proper number of eggs. She set about it at once. She did not 'nest' yet. She simply added another egg each day and then covered them carefully and left them. She would not start sitting on the eggs until she had gathered together enough for a hatch.

My days were freer now. There really wasn't that much for me to do now that the nest was built. I ate and swam a lot, enjoying again the feeling of getting my dives back in shape. Abbie joined me as soon as she had made the morning trip to our nest, and we spent enjoyable times together just talking over our future and our plans for our family.

On the fourth morning that Abbie went to the nest alone, I went off to the pond. I was swimming lazily, feeding on bugs that skimmed along on the surface and dipping down every now and then just to get the feel of the dives, when I heard an awful commotion. Someone was calling my name and that someone was terribly upset.

I looked around and spotted Abbie. She was wild with fear, or anger, or excitement. I couldn't tell which, but I knew that she needed me. I swam quickly to shore and hurried to meet her.

She was all out of breath and tears were running down her cheeks.

"What's wrong?" I asked her, but she was in no condition to be able to talk. Instead she just turned around and headed back toward our nest. I knew that there was no use questioning her further, so I just followed along.

As we neared the nesting site I noticed that the farmer's cows had gathered very near the fence. One of them, a big, placid red and white, was chewing away on a mouthful of straw.

"Look," cried Abbie, and then I saw for myself what had upset Abbie and my eyes widened and my mouth dropped open.

"She's eating our nest," screamed Abbie, and she began to cry harder.

I headed for the cow, with flapping wings and threatening quacks, but she paid no attention to me. She just lowered her head and butted at me gently and went right on chewing.

It was then that I spotted Abbie's three precious eggs, every one of them broken. No wonder Abbie was upset!

I turned from the big monster before me and tried to console Abbie. I didn't know what I could say to comfort her. We had worked so hard on that home. Now it was gone. Gone in a few minutes to a hungry cow. And Abbie's eggs that she had so carefully tucked in each day, that were to be our future family, were smashed on the ground before us. No wonder Abbie was crying. I felt like crying, too.

"Shh-hh," I said to Abbie. "Don't cry. Don't cry."

But Abbie still cried.

"We'll get a new place," I assured her, though I had no idea where that might be. "We'll find a place where the cows can't reach and we'll build again."

Abbie began to sniffle.

"It won't take so long," I kept on. "We know all about nest-building now. We can build much faster than we did before."

She wiped away tears.

"I'll get busy looking right away," I hastened to tell her.

She nodded her head.

We walked away together. I didn't even look back at the munching cow. I was very angry but there was nothing whatever that I could do. To eat our nest was unforgivable, but to smash our nest eggs was criminal. I wanted nothing to do with that cow.

We began our search all over again. There were not many places left to look. At least we had eliminated several sites so we did not have to tramp over that ground again.

We picked a spot that we had likely walked past a good many times. Perhaps we were not as fussy now. Certainly, we had more of a feeling of urgency. The spot was not too far off the path leading to the pond. It was about halfway between the farmyard and the water, and was sheltered by a building that housed our grain. It was high and dry and it was well protected from hawks flying overhead. I think that we both wondered why we hadn't seen it before.

We began building at once. I don't know if it was because we now had some experience or because building materials did not need to be carried as far, but this nest-building went much faster. Soon it was completed and Abbie began to carefully tuck away her egg each day.

I went back to the pond, swam and waited for her to join me. While waiting I talked with other fellows who were also waiting for their mates.

The days passed by, one by one. I sort of lost track of them and then one day Abbie failed to come to the pond.

I swam about waiting and watching and finally, in concern, I decided to go looking for her.

She was not in the yard feeding. I looked all around and did not spot her. Finally I went to our new nest wondering if she had had some misfortune again. There she sat, looking very smug. She was nesting.

"I have eight eggs now," she said. "That is enough for us to care for."

"Eight?" I said, grinning. "Eight. That will be quite enough to care for."

"I think that it will be just right," went on Abbie.

"I think so too."

"You might begin to do some thinking about names," said Abbie, as though the ducklings would be hatching any time now.

I grinned again. "I'll do that," I said. "I'd like to call one of the boys Zackery, if it's okay with you."

She nodded.

"What would you like me to do?" I asked her.

"Nothing. Nothing for now. Later you can take a turn on the

nest when I need to eat."

I agreed.

"When will you want to eat?" I asked her.

She looked at the sky. "Around noon," she said, "and again in the evening."

"You'll be on the nest all night?" I asked.

She nodded again.

"So you won't be sleeping at the barn?"

"Oh, no. The eggs would get cold."

"I'll stay here with you," I promised.

"I'd like that. Thank you."

I went back to the pond then, but I was so excited that I could hardly think straight. I was to be a father soon. Oh, I knew that great responsibilities came along with fatherhood, but there would be pride and pleasure too. I could envision myself and Abbie the first morning that we led our ducklings to the pond. All eight of them. We'd show them off to all our neighbors and I'd teach them all of the things that my parents had taught me. I hoped that the time would pass very quickly, but somehow I knew that it would not. It would seem like a very long time.

In the meantime, I hoped for a warm and pleasant spring, The nights could still be cool and Abbie would spend all of her time on the nest. I did so hope that things would be as pleasant for her as possible.

I did a flip dive to celebrate and struck straight for the bottom of the pond. It was exhilarating. I pointed upward and with swift pushes of my webbed feet I sprang again to the surface.

I was going to be a father!

Chapter Twenty

New Family

The days went slowly by. Some of them were cool as spring storms swept in and the temperature dropped. We had no heavy rains, for which I was thankful, although it did rain off and on. One of the young geese couples had problems with nest flooding. I felt sorry for them and I was glad that Abbie had chosen our nest so carefully. The cold and damp could completely destroy the young lives in the eggs.

Abbie stayed faithfully on the nest and only left it when I was there to relieve her. She went then for a hurried feeding and, on occasion, took a quick dip in the pond. I told her that she should take longer and get some of the kinks out of her back but she just smiled and declared that she was just fine.

Day by day the time went by. We began to see other babies about the farmyard and that only made us more impatient. Three of the hens from the henhouse were already proudly clucking their way around the yard with fluffy balls of yellow chicks, flitting around their feet. The mothers were proud indeed.

One morning as I swam in the pond, dipping and diving, I noticed a duck couple coming toward the water.

It was Mother and Father, and following them was a brand new brood of ducklings, I swam over to greet them and Father beamed his pleasure. There were nine in the bunch—six fellows and three girls. They were a fine looking family and I thought that Father had reason to be proud. Mother was too busy with the new youngsters to have much time to talk, but she smiled at me and asked about Abbie. I assured her that Abbie was fine and all was going well. In a few days we ourselves hoped to be parents, I told her.

"We had a setback in the beginning," I reminded Mother. "First we had difficulty finding a place to build, and then a cow destroyed our first nest and Abbie's first three eggs."

Mother shared our sadness. "That happened to us, our second year," she said. "It's a terrible experience."

"At the time," said Father, "the cow broke six of our seven eggs. We had no way to move the seventh. We had to start all over again. We only raised three young that year."

There was still sorrow in his voice as he thought back.

Then Father turned to his new brood and his eyes sparkled. "And this year we have nine again. Two years in a row, nine."

The children became impatient and Father and Mother had to move on.

I climbed ashore and went to share the good news with Abbie. Besides, she must be in need of a little exercise, I decided. I could take a turn on the nest.

As I waddled up the trail I met another couple leading their young for their first swim. I nodded to them, though I did not know them well. The pride showed in their eyes as they admonished their little ones to stay in line.

Another few days passed. Horace and Fluff came forward with six fluffy ducklings. They, too, joined the increasing number of families on the pond. With each new group, I became more impatient. I did wish that there was some way to speed things up a bit, but Abbie assured me with a smile that there was none.

And then, one day as I neared Abbie, I noticed that her eyes were sparkling even more brightly than usual.

"Shh-hh." she said. "Listen."

I cocked my head and listened. At first I could hear nothing.

"Move closer," said Abbie.

I moved in closer and tipped my head toward the nest. And then I heard it. A soft pecking sound was coming from under Abbie. My eyes lit up.

"Is it time?" I asked incredulously.

"It's time," she answered, her eyes shining.

"When did they start?"

"A few hours ago."

"When will they hatch?"

"It shouldn't take long. From the movement, I think that one of them must be about to break free of the shell anytime."

"Can I see?" I asked breathlessly.

Abbie arose slowly, careful not to disturb any of the eggs. She stepped from the nest and I stepped closer and peered down.

Abbie was right. One small duckling was just ready to break free of the eggshell that had bound him. No, not him—her. A daughter! A brand new daughter! She was beautiful.

"What shall we call her?" I asked, beaming.

"How about Henrietta?" said Abbie.

"Henrietta. That's nice."

I looked around at the other eggs. Most of them had small holes pecked in the side. Some of them were further along than others. Even as I watched, another egg cracked wide open and a small duckling pulled his tucked head from under his wing and blinked at the new world. Then he began to struggle to free himself from the last of the eggshell. I ached to be able to help him.

"A boy," said Abbie.

"A son," I said after her.

We both looked at him in wonder.

"There's your Zack," said Abbie.

I nodded. There were tears in my eyes. I noticed that Abbie had tears in her eyes, too.

I know that they were tears of happiness, but some of them might have been from hurtful memories, too.

"I'd better not let them get cold," said Abbie and moved carefully back to cover our family.

I didn't go back to the pond that day. I stayed with Abbie. It was so exciting to see our family enter the new world one by one. I could hardly wait until they had all arrived and were strong enough to leave the nest. How proud we would be as we marched them forth and began the lessons at the pond.

By the next morning we had seven new babies. Only one of the eggs did not hatch and Abbie removed it from the nest.

We waited until the young ducklings had gotten some strength in their legs and then led from forth.

I was sure that they were just a bit prettier and a bit quicker than any of the other families that I had seen around. They minded beautifully right from the start, and caught on very quickly when they were shown how to strike out with their little webbed feet and how to give their bodies a quick flip that sent them under the water. I swam proudly before them, quacking out my pride and my lessons, happy to show off the family that Abbie and I shared to everyone.

There were five girls and two boys. We called the boys Zack and Linden and the girls Henrietta, Tiny, Miss Fluff, and the two little lookalikes (that even kept their father and mother guessing) Cindy and Mindy.

They were beautiful, obedient children, and I was sure that everyone on the pond and in the farmyard must be envious. At least they would have been had they had time to notice our babies. It seemed that they were all too busy with babies of their own to really pay that much attention to us. I felt badly about that, but I was also too busy with mine to pay much attention to them, so I really couldn't tell if they noticed us much or not. It took one's full time just to care for the family.

Abbie was a good mother and, between the two of us, we got their training under way immediately. Never had I been happier.

I thought back on all of the frustration of the searching out and building a nest—the countless trips with straw and twigs, the deep hurt when the cow ate our property, the re-building. I thought of the many days and nights of sitting on the eggs waiting for the day of hatching to finally come. It had been work. It had taken endurance and dedication, but as I looked around me at my beautiful family I knew that it had all been more than worth it.